Matt Tighe is a speculative fiction writer of horror, sci-fi and fantasy, probably in that order. He is an Australian Shadows Award winner, the recipient of the New England Writers' Centre 2023 Varuna-NEWC Fellowship, and a repeat finalist for the Aurealis and Ditmar Awards. He lives on a small farm in New South Wales with his amazing children, his patient spouse, and too many animals. He is also a professor of environmental science who works on pollution and environmental conservation.

"In a compelling blend of whimsy and weird, Matt Tighe's *Drowning in the Dark and Other Stories* shows us the dark thing behind the door, or over the back fence, through the lens of loss and guilt, each story peppered with people we know and drawn in lines so sharp it takes your breath away. Tighe knows how to spin a yarn; an astounding collection from one of Australia's best short fiction specialists."
—Lee Murray, five-time Bram Stoker Award®-winning author of *Grotesque: Monster Stories*

"Matt Tighe's short fiction is as polished and stark as a bone picked clean in the wilderness, and equally disquieting. These stories will live inside you and confront you in the best possible ways. Tighe is a writer to watch."
—Alan Baxter, award-winning author of *The Gulp* and *Blood Covenant*

Drowning in the Dark and Other Stories

by Matt Tighe

IFWG Publishing International
Gold Coast
www.ifwgpublishing.com

Acknowledgements

I don't know if many people read acknowledgements, but some of those who should be thanked might flip to these pages to see if they got a mention. Here you go, you greedy people!

First and always, thanks to my stalwart Kara, and the kids. Yes, you got the dedication page, and now you are doubling up! It's the least I could do because you deserve it and so much more. Thank you for making my life richer and deeper and real, and putting up with me. I can be a pain. This I know.

My appreciation must also go to my two support and critique groups—the Horror Critters, and the Soup and Cheese Appreciation Club. Always insightful, kind, and funny. A small cross-section of the best of the spec fic community.

My thanks go out to that community as well—it was only a few short years ago I ventured to my first con, and was welcomed with open arms. It took me a long time, but I found my people. You are so very weird.

Pivoting from the mention of weirdness for no particular reason at all… Thank you to Alan Baxter and Lee Murray, who were kind enough to 'blurb' this collection. Your time is valuable, and you gave it generously.

To IFWG boss Gerry, and editor extraordinaire Noel: thank you for taking this work on and being very patient and kind as well as professional. A similar thanks goes to Greg Chapman, who produced a wonderful cover for the collection and bore with me during the process.

Finally, to you, the person reading this (if you are not one of the above): you made it this far! I hope this means you read the book, and I will stretch that hope further—fingers crossed, you enjoyed it.

For my wife Kara, and my kids Kevin, Casey and Maeve.

Table of Contents

Introduction

I was around ten years old when I found a book in our little school library about vampires and werewolves. It was a book of historical accounts, secondhand "true" tales, newspaper reports, old woodcuttings and the like. The library was one room, and there was no librarian. You did the checkout yourself, so there was no one to ask if I should be taking the book out.

I read the whole thing during the hour-and-a-half bus ride home that afternoon, and did not sleep properly for months afterwards. I would wrap my neck in a towel and get under my blankets with a tiny air hole in front of my face, and think of the one account of a dark, skeletal creature who, in the pre-dawn, was found perched on a young woman's windowsill, its eyes glowing red.

I didn't get over my fear. But the days crawled closer to summer, and in western New South Wales that is not a great time to be wrapping yourself in towels and burying yourself under blankets. I decided that creatures of the night were probably still out there, but if I was turned into one then I would at least not be miserable and sweating every night. Maybe it would be cooler out in the dark.

Maybe I would be more comfortable.

Despite my absolute belief there were things *out there*, I couldn't stop myself. Over the next few years I devoured the usual swath of books (if you are reading this, you know), plus some others. I read King, Koontz, Poe, Lovecraft, as well as a raft of pulpy YA and other horror tales, sometimes ploughing through concepts and writing I could not fathom to get to the payoff—the monster, the creature, the thing that I was sure existed, somewhere, in some form. And of course there was Wells, Wyndham, Sturgeon, Le Guin! What if the things they described, the things not just *out there* but the things that *could be*, an alternate past, a branching future, well… Weren't they just dealing in probabilities masquerading as possibilities? Maybe even certainties, *somewhere, some when*?

This is my first collection, and I believe everything in it. The events, the people, the creatures, are not real. But they could be, or they might be, or one day may be, in some form, in some fashion. Some of these beliefs are bleak. Most have a kernel of hope, or a hint of bittersweet perseverance that people display, even when things are absolutely hopeless. Maybe this is really what I mean when I say I believe all my own stories—that despite everything, we persist.

I hope you enjoy the tales that follow. And if you find some, or most of them, dark, remember—sometimes there is comfort in giving in to the dark, if just for a little while.

A Good Big Brother

Dad says he is going to teach me how to use the gun. Mum has red, watery eyes as she chews on her toast, but she nods when I look at her.

"It's a grown-up thing you need to learn, honey," she says. "And with the baby coming you are going to need to do some more grown-up things. You will be a big brother soon." She smiles but it's only a little one that doesn't make the crinkles next to her eyes. "Dad will teach you how to be careful."

Dad gives a funny little huff—it is one of his grown-up noises that I don't really understand. It looks like his eyes are a bit red too, but he goes into the kitchen before I can tell if he has been crying like Mum.

"I heard some noises last night," I say.

Neither of them looks at me straight away, but I can tell they are listening by how still they get. That's another thing adults do—they go still when you ask them something hard. Maybe it helps them think of the answer.

"I heard it too, kiddo," Dad says.

"There was a loud bang," I say. It's not what I really want to say, but I can't find the words. It feels too big.

"Yes, honey," Mum says. "But it had nothing to do with us."

"Oh," I say.

I take a bite of my toast. Mum makes the bread, and it is okay, but the toast has honey, which makes it better. We have lots of honey. Dad has beehives up in the top paddock, behind the big trees. Dad likes to put the honey in his tea, and when he does, he smiles and tells Mum she can't have any because of the baby. He likes to tease her like that. Mum always laughs a bit, but I think she is sad that there is no sugar anymore. I don't mind. I like the honey better.

"We will start after breakfast," Dad says, and I think of the gun.

I don't like it. I know what guns do. I saw.

We are standing down in the front paddock. There are some big trees here, like up the back, but no bees. My arms are sore from holding the gun. I haven't shot it—Dad says it's too noisy. We are just practising aiming and using the bolt action.

"Do you understand?" Dad asks again. I don't know how many times he has asked, but it seems like a lot.

I nod. He keeps looking at me, so I point.

"That's the safety."

"And what do we know about the safety?"

"That we must use it, but we can't trust it."

Dad goes to speak again, but I know what he is going to say so I get in first.

"And the gun is always loaded, even when we know it is not. And the only time you point it at something is when you are going to shoot it. And that…"

"Yes?" he asks, his voice soft.

"If I hear the bells, and if you or Mum are not there, I am to get the gun and point it at the gate. Just like you showed me. If I see something move, I shoot."

Dad nods.

"I don't like it," I blurt. I'm holding the gun under one arm, like I'm supposed to, and I touch the dark barrel with one finger. "It doesn't feel right." It's not what I really want to say. I want to say it feels alive—that it feels like something that might twist around and bite me, but that would sound silly.

Dad sighs and kneels down next to me.

"Listen, buddy, I know this is tough. But I have to tell you something that is going to be even harder. Things are different now."

"You mean like how I can't see my friends?" I ask, but his eyes slide away. That's another grown-up thing, but I know what this one means. It means Dad won't say what he is really thinking.

"Kind of," he says, and then he stops for a long time.

The gun is getting heavy. I'm about to ask him if I can put it down when he starts talking again.

"You are going to be a big brother soon," he says. He smiles a little bit, but it looks sad. It looks like the smile he gives Mum when he puts his hand on her round tummy. "And there might come a time when you…" Dad pauses and has a funny little cough. When he looks at me again his eyes are watery. "You might have to do some things you don't like. If you do, I want you to remember that no matter how bad it feels, if Mum or me say it's okay, then you just have to do it."

"I don't understand," I say.

The gun feels really heavy. It feels much heavier than it should. I wish I could stop touching it.

"Oh, kiddo, I don't think you could understand, not right now. Just remember, if we say it is okay, you need to do it."

Mum tucks me in. She does that every night, like I'm a little kid.

"I'll be a big brother soon," I say, and she nods without looking at me. She is not paying attention.

"Mum!" I say, and she looks at me.

"Hmmm?"

"I said I'll be a big brother soon. You don't need to tuck me in."

She frowns. "Really?" she says. "Why the grumps?"

I bite my lip. Dad wants me to do grown-up things. I've been thinking and thinking about it, and I've decided I want them to know that I know. That it is a grown-up thing, a big brother thing to know, and I know it.

"I saw what happened," I say, all in a rush.

Mum doesn't say anything straight away, but I can see her hands curl up, gripping my blanket very hard. She doesn't ask what I saw.

"Sweetie," she says after a bit. "That wasn't really Mr Reynolds.

You know how we talked about that? How people aren't really themselves if they have the virus? If they are sick?"

"It still looked like him," I say, but it didn't. Not really.

I had woken to the bells ringing, and then shouting. Dad had put bars on my window, drilling them in with the big drill back when the electricity worked, but I could still see down the drive, right down to the front gate. Dad had put a big lock on the gate and the fence was high on each side. It didn't used to be, but when things started to get bad, Dad had spent a lot of money to have some men come out and make the fence higher and put in the gate with thick iron bars. When they had finished Dad had strung bells through the gate, and they jangled if anyone tried to open it, or even if the wind was strong.

I saw the flickering, jumping light of Dad's torch, and I heard the bells ringing, and there was Mr Reynolds standing at the front gate. Mr Reynolds lived a little way down the road, a bit closer to town. He was older and lived by himself, but he was nice. He would always smile and wave when we drove past, and he dropped Easter eggs in the letterbox every year. But he didn't look the same and Dad stood right back, yelling at Mr Reynolds to get away, to not try to open the gate. Mr Reynolds did not even seem to hear him. The torchlight flickered over his arms and, with my face pressed against the window, I could see they had the green and grey bumpy look that Dad said meant someone was sick. His face was okay, but there was something wrong with his mouth. It hung open really wide, wider than I thought a mouth could open. He made some funny noises, puffing noises like he was out of breath, and tried to push the gate open. The bells rang again, loud and sharp.

The light jumped a bit and then steadied right on Mr Reynolds. There was a bang and Mr Reynolds's head changed shape, like when you squish modelling clay. It seemed to push out to one side, and something wet sprayed through the torchlight into the darkness. He fell.

It was quiet for a bit. I heard some soft crunching footsteps going down the drive and then Mum's voice.

"Was he infected?" she asked, her voice shaking.

"Yeah," Dad replied. They were silent, and then he spoke again. "Go back inside. I'll get the gloves and move him away."

I heard Mum coming back, and Dad moving around in the dark, huffing and grunting. The noises stopped after a while, but I kept looking out into the dark for a long time.

Mum is looking at me.

"It's okay, Mum," I say. "I know it wasn't really him."

She nods quickly and gives me a little smile, but her hands are still gripping my blanket really tight.

Mum and Dad are fighting, but even I can tell it's really just because Mum is scared. I think Dad is scared too, but he is trying not to be.

"We've been over this," he says.

They are standing outside near the front door. He has his backpack on. The sun is low, and it is getting hard to see his face. They don't notice me.

"We need medicine. Antibiotics, bandages, and other stuff. I'd be happier if we had more nappies."

"God, we can use the old cloth ones! I'll rip up some sheets!"

Dad sighs. "You know the nappies are only something I'll grab if I see them. But we need other things, and who knows when I'll get a chance to go after the birth?"

"The birth could be any moment!" Mum almost shouts, and Dad frowns.

"I know that!" he snaps, and then rubs one hand over his face. "I know that," he repeats quietly. "And you know I would've gone the other night, but after Reynolds…"

Mum's shoulders slump a bit, and she makes a little hiccupping sound.

"It's just so close now. And town is dangerous."

"I know, honey. But I've done the trip, what, a dozen times? It will be okay. There is hardly anyone left anyway."

Mum nods glumly. I wish I could hug her, but they still haven't noticed me. I'll just have to be helpful. I'll have to be a grown-up.

I look at her big tummy. She has one hand resting on it lightly. I'll have to be a good big brother.

I am being shaken. I open my eyes, but it is still dark. I think I make a sound, but I'm not sure.

"Honey," Mum says. "Honey, wake up." Her voice sounds funny, like she is sucking in deep breaths between the words.

"Mum?" I ask, and sit up. There is a little bit of orange light from the candle Mum is holding. Her hand is shaking and big shadows jump across the walls of my room.

"Honey, the baby is coming."

I don't know what to say. I know what she means. Mum and Dad have told me what will happen—they call it a "home birth" when they talk about it. I try to think about all that they said as we sat at the table, but I had not listened very much. It was a bit gross.

"Where's Dad?" I say, and Mum sucks in a big breath.

In the flickering light I see her put one hand on her belly, high up, and wince.

"He isn't back." She stops talking and starts panting. After what seems like a long time, she drops her hand and smiles a little. "He won't be long. It's not even dawn yet. And I've got everything ready." She frowns. "The contractions are coming fast."

I don't know what that means, but I don't think she is really talking to me.

I push the covers back and get up.

"What do we do?" I say.

Mum has put extra sheets—old ones—on the floor in the big front room. It is where the wood heater is, where she keeps the water hot. She has a pile of towels and old sheets in a heap nearby. She has been laying there for a long time now, and she is holding my hand tightly. At first it frightened me because the orange candlelight flickered across her face, making her eyes deep shadows and her open mouth a black hole when she moaned. Now she looks grey. Everything does. It is still night, but everything is getting that funny no-colour that comes just before the sun comes up.

"I don't think it will be much longer," she says, her face all sweaty. She tries to smile, but she winces and sucks in a big breath instead.

I really want to cry but I can't. Mum needs me.

She grunts and squeezes my hand. She has been doing that a lot. Earlier I told her she was hurting me and she started to cry—loud, shaky cries. After that I didn't say, even when she squeezed extra hard.

All of a sudden she screams really loud.

"Mum!" I yell. I'm really scared.

"It's okay," she pants. "This is normal."

I don't believe her. This can't be normal.

"It's almost over," she says, and grits her teeth.

I hope she is right.

And then the bells on the gate start jangling.

"Get the gun!" Mum grunts, and then squeezes her eyes shut. "Get the gun and get ready!"

The gun lives by the front door. I know what she means. It is what Dad talked about.

"Can't you do it?" I ask.

The bells jangle again, and I hear the gate rattle.

"I can't!" she yells, and then screams again.

I let go of her hand and run to the door. I snatch up the gun and step out the front.

The sun is not up yet and everything is grey shadows. It is hard to see down the drive. Everything is just soft lines and shapes. Something, or someone, is pushing on the gate. It is supposed to be locked, but I can see it moving, opening.

"Someone is coming!" I try to call back inside, but Mum screams again.

I put the gun up to my shoulder and look through the sight. All I can see is someone moving, grey against grey. There is a puffing, huffing sound, like someone out of breath.

"Mum?" I ask. My voice has gone all wobbly and soft. "What if it's Dad?"

I keep looking through the sight. Everything is blurry, and I think I am crying. Someone is coming. The puffing sound is getting louder.

"Mum?" I ask again, and then I hear crying.

It is not Mum. It is the crying of a baby, and it is very loud. I want to look back, but I know I can't. I keep looking through the sight of the gun. My arms are starting to shake.

I can feel my finger tightening on the trigger. I don't want to shoot, but Mum and the baby are just there. If it was Dad coming, would he have jangled the bells? Would he call out? Should I call out? All I know is I need to be a good big brother. I need to do the right thing.

"Mum? What do I do?" I whisper.

I can't see properly through my tears. A face swims into view in the sight of the gun. I can't see who it is. All I can hear is the baby crying—my little brother or sister.

I hear Mum take a big watery breath.

"It's okay," she says.

It is what Dad said they would say. I pull the trigger.

Monstrous Behaviour

I'm trying to clean up from one of the practice bouts but my mop is really only pushing blood around the Arena floor. A good mop is hard to find.

"Becca," Entwistle calls. "Perhaps you could take a short break?"

That's a surprise. Entwistle likes a clean Arena. But now he is looking down at me from the VIP platform, pale cheekbones and natty pinstripe suit like normal, and there is something in his eyes that I don't quite get. I shake my head and he frowns, his giant bushy eyebrows drawing down.

"I'm almost done," I say.

Entwistle turns back to his guest. The man is dressed in an army uniform with lots of shiny medals, and he is standing ramrod straight, but he is also old, and seems kind of soft. He has two younger, fitter offsiders, but one of them looks fidgety. I know that look. Maybe he had heard about monsters, but until today, he had no reason to try and make them fit with the shape of his world. I almost feel sorry for that one, but I can see that Mr Entwistle is worried, and that makes me uneasy. Entwistle is a great boss, and he looks after all the monsters. He makes sure the ghouls only get prime beef cuts, and he even lets the living dolls do their weird self-oiling thing when they are on break, which is kind of gross if you think about it too much.

"So," the old army guy says, "can we get on with this?"

Entwistle sighs. "I'm telling you it's a mistake, General. You don't want a Frankenstein. A Sphinx will beat a Frankenstein, hands down, every time."

I think I know why Entwistle is entertaining this guy. The Arena is not exactly legal. It's what Entwistle calls an open secret, and I get that. I've seen more than one big fat cat in the audience, placing bets. Sometimes I know their faces from the TV, or those stupid ads on my Facebook feed. This guy I don't know, but I can guess he has more power than our pale, sweaty mayor. And he wants something.

"Really?" the General says, and raises one grey eyebrow. It's not as bushy as Entwistle's, but it's no malnourished caterpillar. "That's not what our analysts say."

"Frankensteins are brutes. Sphinxes like puzzles and riddles as much as they like eating people. They are thinkers."

That's not anywhere near the truth, and I think both Charlie and the Lady would both be pretty upset to hear it, but I get it. Entwistle is trying to avoid a mess, and by the sounds of it, maybe trying to stop Charlie being drafted.

The General smiles, and it's not a nice smile. I live with monsters, so I should know.

"We've been through this. You can show me what you've got, or I can take it all."

Entwistle shoots a quick glance at me and I turn away to empty my bucket. I don't want him to see the worry on my face. All the dark corners of the world are now lit up by the glow from smartphones and computer screens, and no one, and no thing, can hide from YouTube forever. Places like this, shelters like this, are few and far between. The monsters have nowhere else to go. Not anywhere safe, anyway. I know I don't.

"Fine," Entwistle says, and waves a hand.

The gate opens and the Lady walks into the Arena—stalks, really, like the cat she kind of is. She stops and crouches, her body rippling with muscles, her giant wings folded against her golden flanks, her beautiful face haughty and unmoving.

A moment later the Frankenstein (actually, a Frankenstein's *monster*—Charlie can be a bit pedantic about it) comes bursting through his door. He roars and presents himself, chest bared, all thick black stitching and mismatched limbs. He has one huge arm that is almost dragging on the ground, and he roars again as he sees the Sphinx across the Arena. I try to hide my grin. Charlie, who loves Gilbert and Sullivan and is always trying to get someone, anyone, to form an improv group on nights off, is certainly making a show of it.

The Lady crouches as still as only a waiting cat can. Charlie charges, roaring again, and hits her as hard as he can—or tries to. She flaps her wings once and leaps straight up into the air, and Charlie stands there, a puzzled expression replacing the rage on his horrible hatchet-job of a face as he stares at the space she had just occupied. And then the Sphinx strikes as she hovers there, her giant wings thrumming. She does not bite or kick or even roar. She simply reaches down with one giant paw, claws extended, and plucks the stitching that runs around Charlie's neck. Yanks it, actually. And, well, the rest is quick but messy. Someone is going to be busy with sewing for a few days, and I hope it's not me. Charlie can be a real ass about the cross-stitching.

The General looks a bit nonplussed, and shoots a glance at Entwistle that is perhaps a little suspicious.

"So it's the Sphinx," he says. Entwistle sighs.

"I only have the one. And she will only do your bidding if you answer a riddle correctly. Get it wrong and she will eat you."

The General frowns.

"You know the deal, Entwistle. I want a monster for my new program. Now, either show me what you've got that can beat the Sphinx, or I'm shutting this place down." He smiles again. "Maybe you and the Sphinx will need to be a package deal."

I am gripping my broom handle so tightly I think I've gotten some splinters. The General is lucky the monsters are all out of hearing as well as sight. None of them would take kindly to Entwistle being threatened. I think even the Lady is looking a little unimpressed.

Entwistle looks away from the General and once again gives me that funny look. This time I understand. Of course. He has planned this like one of the bouts—scripted down to the finest detail. I look at this army man who has so casually threatened my boss, and I give a little nod.

"So," the General says. "Do you have something that can beat the Sphinx?"

Entwistle seems to hesitate. "Well, I do have a Tulpa."

"What's that?" the General asks.

"It's a manifestation of will. Often associated with eastern religions, but the one I have is inherited."

"Dangerous? Controllable?"

"Well, yes," Entwistle says. "But you need to understand, General, that once a Tulpa is released, it will not stop until its objective is met."

"But that sounds perfect," the General says. He is even smiling a little.

Entwistle shakes his head. "Yes. I know how it sounds. But a Tulpa interprets its own success."

The General shakes his head. "That just sounds like a matter of clear orders. Come on, let's see this thing."

Entwistle looks at me, and I see the faintest flicker of a smile as he nods. I don't feel like smiling. I don't like extra mess.

The Sphinx is still crouching in the arena. There is a lot of blood and embalming fluid on the floor now, but Charlie has been dragged away, playing dead no doubt as enthusiastically as he played the enraged brute. I hate trying to clean up embalming fluid. It stinks so much.

"Should I climb down?" I ask Entwistle.

He shakes his head.

"Why bother? I was hoping to avoid this, but it seems we are at an impasse."

I nod, avoiding the curious gazes of the old General and his young sidekicks.

"An objective?"

Entwistle frowns in thought, his comic eyebrows drawing down for a moment before popping back up.

"Perhaps just a brief show of the Tulpa's capability. If the General agrees, of course."

The General frowns a little, first at Entwistle, and then at me. I get the distinct feeling he is not used to actually recognising underlings such as myself as anything close to human. Which is kind of amusing, given the situation.

"Yes," the General says slowly. "But I don't suppose I need to remind you of what would happen to this place if something happens to me." He pauses, eyeing me and smiling. "What would happen to all of you."

I don't say anything, and neither does Entwistle. I do feel a little sorry for the General (and his sidekicks), but only a little. I can recognise a monster when I see one.

"Well?" the General says. I look at him, and after a moment, his pompous smile curdles at the edges. I know what he is seeing. I've seen it in the mirror. My face and my body are suddenly partially obscured by a misty substance that has started to coalesce in front of me. It feels like sweat cooling on my skin. It's funny but not, you know, *ha ha* funny. There is no pain, and I don't have to make any conscious effort. I simply decide it is happening, and it is. In a moment the grey mist has formed into something like the smoky outline of a person, wavering and shifting in front of me. It does not take direction from me now, but it did as it formed. I am as curious as anyone to see what it will do with its limited instructions, but I know two things that Entwistle also knows—the Tulpa also likes it here at the Arena, and the Tulpa always surprises.

The misty form glides forward, shifting and shimmering, twisting its ethereal limbs like it is dancing towards the General. One of the uniformed sidekicks (the non-fidgety one) steps forward, drawing a handgun, and I find it in my heart to finally feel properly sorry for him. He looks scared but determined.

The Tulpa slides into him and he shrieks and drops the gun. That's good. Unlike some of the monsters, I'm not bulletproof. He drops to his knees, holding his head as the Tulpa slides out the other side of him. He falls down, and I know he is dead before he hits the floor. It won't be just beef for the ghouls tonight, I suppose.

The General backs away and throws a terrified glance at Entwistle.

"What do you think you are doing?"

Entwistle shrugs.

"I think your analysts maybe got more than a few things wrong."

"You have no idea of the shitstorm that will rain down on you if you do this."

Entwistle smiles a little.

"Oh, I'm not worried. The Tulpa is nothing if not creative."

The second sidekick—the one that looked so afraid earlier— suddenly throws both hands straight up in the air, like he is being mugged. In truth, it's probably the smartest thing he could've done. Much better than running. The Tulpa sways, considering him for a moment, and then continues towards the General.

"You can't do this!" he screams. His nasty smile has finally fled. Given the General's threats, I'm also very curious to see what the Tulpa will do.

The Tulpa reaches the General and sways to and fro in front of him, just like it is thinking. Maybe it is. Once I release it, I have no magic window into what is going on in that smoky head.

Finally, it reaches out with one wispy hand. The General shrieks and shrinks back, but not far or fast enough. The Tulpa's hand reaches into his chest. The General's eyes roll up until all I can see are the whites, and I think he is going to collapse. He surprises me, though. He just stands there shaking, while his remaining bodyguard stands next to him, his hands still thrust up to the sky. After a long moment (which I'm sure is much longer for the General), the Tulpa pulls its hand back out, and I see it is missing one smoky finger. *Ah.*

The Tulpa shimmers for a moment and then dissipates, the grey smoke of its body flowing away like it has been caught in a strong breeze. There is a long, pregnant silence. The bodyguard looks around and then hesitantly lowers his hands. His face goes a little pink.

The General takes several deep breaths and then straightens. He is pale, and his eyes are definitely a little too wide, and a little too darting, but he has recovered surprisingly quickly. Maybe his training has kicked in or something.

"You're done, Entwistle. This place is done," he snaps, and then pauses, glancing about. Nothing happens, and he suddenly looks more confident.

"Let's see how your misfits fare against a platoon or two of my…" He drifts off, and his eyes roll upwards again so all I can see are the whites. It is like he is trying to look inside his own head. I wonder if he sees anything.

Slowly he seems to recover, and as his eyes come good he raises one hand and rubs at his chest. He stares at me, his face suddenly sweaty.

I nod at the question I see there.

"The Tulpa has a finger on your heart, General," I say. "It usually surprises." I smile widely. "So—*surprise!*"

Not long after that the General leaves. There is no more bluster from him, no more threats. The Tulpa has him in the palm of its hand. Well, kind of.

Mr Entwistle looks at me.

"Thank you, Becca. I know you don't like to let it out unless you have to. How can I show my gratitude?"

I smile. I like Entwistle. I like my home. And I even like my job. Mostly.

"Can I have a new mop?"

Memories Of Blue

My slippers are blue. I don't remember buying them. It is just a little thing, really, but there are so many little things like it. They make one big thing, all of them together. I think I have thought of this before, but I am not sure. I shake my head.

"What are you looking at, Dad?"

There is a girl next to me. She has dark hair and green eyes, and she is ten years old, grinning as she shows me her new sun dress—the blue one with the yellow flowers. It is her favourite. I blink, and she is a grown woman, frowning at me, a crease of worry between her eyes.

"Lacy?" I ask. I see the hurt in her eyes before she banishes it with a faded echo of a ten-year-old's smile.

"Yeah, Dad." She sits next to me. I am in an armchair, in a room. For a moment I panic, but then I see my things on the dresser. Marjorie is there in her frame—my Marjorie, in her wedding dress, so happy, so alive. She looks so much like the woman sitting with me, but I know it is not her. Marjorie is dead. Dead and gone, years ago. It does not come as a shock. I am grateful for that, at least. Feeling that pain again, fresh, that would not be a little thing.

"How are you?" Lacy, my Lacy, asks me.

"Oh," I say. "You know." My response feels familiar. This could be something I have said before. She nods and smiles. I am glad she knows. I am glad one of us does.

"Are they treating you okay?"

"No complaints," I say. This, too, has a familiar shape to it as it passes my lips. I do not want to burden this woman with my ramblings. But of course, it is not some woman—it is Lacy, my Lacy, with the green eyes and her mother's smile. My accomplished Lacy, with such smarts, who has gone so far beyond the world I understand. My gaze falls. My slippers are blue.

"Blue," I say. I do not mean to. She frowns. "Remember your blue dress? With the yellow flowers?"

Her smile is so much like her mother's it hurts. "Oh, I loved that dress," she says. "My favourite colours. And it was the last thing Mum ever bought me." Then she looks at me, biting her lip.

"The doctors say you are not so well these days. That things are…" She swallows, and I think she might cry, but then she takes a big watery breath instead. "I've been working on something. I'd like to try it out. Maybe tomorrow?"

I nod, and the woman gets up. She kisses me on the forehead before she leaves, but I don't watch her go. I am looking down. My slippers are blue.

There is a woman, and she is doing something to me.

"Who are you?" I ask. I raise one hand to grab at my head. "What are you doing?"

The woman grabs my hand. I try to pull away but she lifts my hand quickly and presses it to her lips.

"Dad!" Lacy says, and I stop trying to pull away. She nods and lets go. "Dad, we talked about this. Do you remember?"

I reach up, slowly, and this time Lacy does not stop me. My fingers slip over something hard and rectangular just behind my ear.

"This," I say, trying to think of Lacy's words. It is so hard. "This might help me?"

She nods. "I hope so. Do you remember?"

I do not like it when people ask me to remember. It does not hurt, but it does hurt at the same time, to have to sift through all those scattered, broken images and words with no meaning—all those missing little things. But it is my Lacy asking, so I try.

"Quant…" I start.

"Quantum neural aligner," a woman next to me says. I have been looking at my things on the dresser. At Marjorie. I don't know why this woman is here. My slippers are blue. My daughter loves her blue dress.

L acy smiles at me.

"The staff say you are doing better."

"No complaints," I say, and then I smile. It feels good. Lacy looks surprised, and that feels even better. My hand drifts up to my ear.

"They didn't ask…" I begin, and my daughter nods.

"I told them it is a hearing aid. It looks like one. I made sure of that."

"What does it do?"

She looks at me with that slight crease between her eyes—so much like her mother.

"Do you remember what I do?"

I nod. "Of course. You are a scientist. You work at the university."

Her frown deepens a little. "An experimental physicist, yes. But I work for MemCorp, a private company."

I shrug. I was sure she worked at the university, but it is just a little thing. And it is just one little thing. I still have no complaints.

"That device is still experimental. I would get fired if anyone knew I had it. If you had it."

"What does it do?"

Lacy's crease eases and she smiles a little. She has always been so smart.

"It's a quantum neural aligner. It works on something called the Branching Cats Theory. You are entangled with multiple expressions of you, in a quantum sense. We all are. This boosts that link."

I stare at her. For a moment she is a girl—just a little girl, grinning in her favourite dress. And then she is Lacy again, Lacy who works at the university. She takes my hand.

"It's a memory photocopier, Dad. In a quantum sense, there are other places, other versions of you. Ones who are maybe not so…sick. I am borrowing from them. You are borrowing from them."

She smiles. "You can have it all back. We can have it back."

I smile because she is smiling, but I know I can't have it all back. Not really. I can't have Marjorie, and I can't have my little girl dancing in her blue dress.

Lacy is not smiling anymore.

"It's nothing to worry about," I say. I try not to sound annoyed, or afraid. My mind is clear. My memories are clear. It is the world that is the problem.

"They say you are not sleeping," she says quietly. "They say you say things that are not right. That you are not just forgetful anymore."

"Give me a break!" I say. "Last week everything I said was not right."

She nods, looking thoughtful. "That could be it, yes. Just a period of adjustment." She looks hopeful, but then sighs.

"Humour me. Answer some questions?"

I nod, even though I do not really want to.

"Who am I?"

I almost laugh. "My Lacy," I say, ignoring how hard this question would have been a week ago.

"And where do I work?"

"The university—no, wait, some private company. Mimco? Something like that."

She frowns. I hope she will not press. It's not like it was, not like broken images and gaps in my mind. I have no memory of Mimco, or whatever it is, but I can see the university clearly. Green lawns, sandstone walls, a smiling Lacy at the cafeteria with three steaming coffees in front of her. That was not so long ago, really.

"And where are you?"

"I'm in the old folks' home."

"And my favourite dress when I was younger?"

"That's easy," I say. "Your green sundress. It had red flowers."

She suddenly looks too pale, too concerned. She opens her

mouth but I hold up a forestalling hand. I have a question of my own, one I did not want to ask the staff. They would not pay attention. They would think it was a little thing. But this is my Lacy, so I ask.

"Lacy. Where is your mother? Where are her things? She was here yesterday."

There is a woman sitting next to me. She is crying. She is holding my hand. My face feels wet as well. I wonder if I have been crying. I wonder what I might have to cry about.

"Hello," I say. "Are you alright? Am I?"

She squeezes my hand and lifts the other to wipe at her face. There is something in that hand, something small and hard and rectangular.

"Is that mine?" I ask. I do not know why I ask.

"No, Dad," the woman says, and then smiles through her tears. "I thought it was, but not yet. I have more work to do."

I look down. My slippers are blue.

"Remember your blue dress, Lacy?" I ask. "The one with the yellow flowers?"

Wriggleteeth

There was something wrong with the cat. It had taken it three goes to get through the gap under the stairs, bumping its head and weaving side to side in its attempts. It was probably hungry. Usually it seemed fine. Brody had seen it around, especially at night, outside his bedroom window. He didn't think anyone owned it. He would feed it and get a collar for it and eventually it could sleep on his bed. His parents wouldn't care. They wouldn't notice.

A cat would be good. Back in the city he had friends at school and his Dad came home at dinner time. In the city his Mum smiled more. Here it was different, and not *good* different.

He wriggled into the gap beside the back stairs. It was a tight fit, and a piece of splintery wood got him down his side, scratching through his shirt, but the cat was kind of fat and Brody was pretty skinny. He got through okay in the end, even holding the big piece of steak from the fridge.

"Here, puss puss puss," Brody whispered. It was dark under the house, but the cat was kind of bright orange and might not have gone in too far. He should be able to spot it. He lay on his belly and held the meat in front of him. He waved it around.

"Puss puss!"

Nothing happened. Maybe he should have got some tuna — cats like fish. Or milk. He should have got some milk and put it in a bowl outside.

He moved in further, kind of flopping on his belly, holding the meat so it didn't get too dirty. It was hard going, but it wasn't far.

There was a column of bricks a few more flops in, the first of a bunch that went back into the dark and that held up the floor or something. He squirmed forward, sneezing at the fine dust going up his nose, and when he got level with the bricks he saw it.

It was lying on its side, facing away and into the darkness, but it raised its head and looked back at him. It meowed. It sounded sad. Maybe it was sick.

"Want some food?" Brody whispered, and tossed the steak in front of it. The cat sniffed it and then laid its head back down on the ground.

"Hey, cat! Want some food?" Brody hissed, but it didn't look at him. It was breathing kind of fast. He shuffled forward on his belly a bit farther until he could see more of it.

"Are you having babies?" he asked. Mrs Sorensen had had a baby. Brody's mother had opened the door of their apartment back in the city one night and their neighbour had been standing there, her small face scrunched up while she did funny breathing like the cat, and Brody's mother had taken her to the hospital. Plus, the cat wasn't interested in the food, even though she was fat. A kitten would be good. His mother might like a kitten—they were pretty cute.

The cat lay there, panting. Brody wriggled closer, but then stopped. There was a black thing on the cat's neck, a thick glistening worm, or maybe it was a leech. Brody had seen leeches before in *The Book of Bugs* at his old school. They drank blood and got fat from it. This one was going to drink the cat's blood. Was probably already drinking it. Maybe that was what was wrong.

He thought about trying to pull it off, but he didn't think he could touch it. What if it bit him? What if it drank his blood?

"I don't know what to do," he whispered to the cat. It meowed again.

The leech moved. A little bulge ran down its length, and the back end of it rose and wiggled in the air.

And then it got shorter. At first Brody thought it was bunching up, pushing itself forward, getting in behind the fur, but then he saw it was doing more than that. It was disappearing inside the cat. He didn't know leeches did that.

The cat raised its head again and looked at him, but now it seemed fine. There was a spot of blood on the fur of its neck where the leech had gone in, but she had stopped her funny panting, and as he watched the cat got up and stretched lazily. It came to him and rubbed its head against his arm.

"That's a good cat," Brody said. "You okay?"

The cat purred and trotted past him and out towards the back yard.

"Mum, can leeches hurt you?"

Brody wanted to ask Dad, but it was bedtime and Dad wasn't home. Mum looked tired. They had had pizza for dinner, but it had been almost cold and the cheese had been a bit waxy.

"What, dear?" she asked as she pulled his blanket up.

"Leeches? Do they get inside you?"

She frowned a little. "Hmmm? I don't know. I think they just drink blood. I don't think they hurt. I've never had one, but I guess they might be about. We aren't in the city anymore."

She patted him absently on the arm.

"Can we get a cat?" he asked. He didn't mean to. It just kind of popped out.

"Oh, I don't know. Maybe."

She kissed him on the forehead and went out, leaving the door open a bit. When she was gone Brody got up and went to the window, but he couldn't see the cat anywhere.

The bad thing with Mitchell happened at recess the next day. Brody had been thinking about the cat and the leech, and had maybe not paid attention to the looks he was getting.

Mitchell pushed him over in the grass.

"Your dad is an arsehole!" the bigger boy hissed, crouching down next to Brody. "My dad says so."

"My dad is your dad's boss," Brody replied. Mitchell must not know—he wouldn't push Brody over if he knew. He started to get up and Mitchell gave him a rabbit punch on the top of his head. He had done that before, and not just to Brody, and he always yelled 'Rabbitsies!' when he did it and laughed like it was funny.

But this one was hard and really hurt, and Mitchell didn't yell out anything. Instead, he gave a little puff of breath like he had tried to hit really hard.

"Ow!" Brody yelled. His eyes filled with tears and he put one hand to the top of his head. He sat down and looked up at the other boy.

There was a pause. Mitchell looked around. Some of the other kids who were watching moved away, in case a teacher had heard. After a moment of nothing, Mitchell stepped forward.

"Go back to the city," he said, and pushed Brody backwards. Hard.

Brody hadn't expected it. His head hit something and his teeth came together with a hollow *clunk* that went right up through his jaw and into his eyeballs. He sat up slowly, and when he touched the back of his head his hand came away red with blood.

The fat cat came back late that afternoon while Brody was sitting in the back yard, except it wasn't fat anymore. It was kind of skinny. It meowed at him and then climbed the little poplar tree in the corner that looked like a pole with a few pretend branches.

"Hey you," Brody said. His head hurt, but it was getting better. He had told the teacher he had fallen off the monkey bars. Mitchell didn't like him, but being a tattler wasn't going to make things better. He had been given a cold pack for his head and got to sit quietly instead of doing maths. He had also been given an "incident note" to give his parents, but he had put it at the bottom of the garbage bin in the kitchen.

He hadn't been watching, but suddenly the cat dropped down from the tree. The grass was long because Dad hadn't mowed it, and it rustled backwards and forwards fast where the cat was.

"What have you got?" Brody asked, and walked over. He did it slowly, because his head still hurt.

The cat had a bird. Brody didn't know much about birds, but

he had seen lots of these ones. His mother called them top-knots, and they were like a pigeon, with a little sticky-up crest at the tops of their heads. Sometimes they would fly really fast across the yard and their wings would make a kind of whirring sound.

The cat had this one by the neck. The bird rolled one round orange eye up at Brody and flapped a wing weakly. The cat put a paw on the wing and growled softly.

"Shoo! Shoo!" Brody told the cat, and waved his arms. The cat ignored him, so he squatted down and went to push the cat away.

It lifted its head from the bird and hissed. Brody sucked in his breath and pulled his hands back as if from something hot.

When the cat had opened its mouth, instead of teeth it had a bunch of thin, squirming black leeches coming out of its gums. They moved backwards and forwards in the air, blindly wriggling this way and that, the ends of each wet and red.

Brody took a few steps back and the cat lowered its head back to the bird. The wing flapped once more, very slowly, and then stopped. After a minute Brody moved forward a bit, just a couple of little steps.

The bird stared up at the sky with its one orange eye, and Brody could tell it was dead. And it looked kind of…*flat*. Shrunken. The cat looked back up at him and purred. It still looked skinny, thin in its face and along its back where its spine poked against the skin in knobs, but its belly now pushed out in a round little bulge.

Want some food? Brody thought, and felt queasy.

He didn't want to bring the cat inside anymore.

It was not exactly Mitchell the next day, but that didn't make it better. Brody was heading into the toilet block when someone tripped him and he fell on the concrete. He took the skin off both of his knees, one of them bad enough to leave a smear of blood on the concrete. He sat up and grabbed at both of the injuries, one knee in each hand. It didn't help.

He got up and turned around, blinking the wetness away from his eyes. Mitchell stood over by the big pepper tree with two other boys. One—a boy named Hamish—laughed, and then the three of them ducked around the tree and out of sight.

Brody limped into the toilet block and tried to wash the scrapes on his knees. It stung, but when he got the blood and a couple of chunky pebbles off the raw bits they didn't look too bad. He could bear it, although he cried a bit in one of the toilet cubicles. Finally he managed to stop. At least the day was nearly over.

They weren't done, though. When the bell rang for the end of school, Brody's school bag was gone. The hook he hung it on outside the classroom was empty. Mitchell and his two friends came out and grabbed their own bags, and when they went past they all snickered. Mitchell pushed him, and he stumbled forward into the wall.

"Where is my bag?" he asked, trying to keep his voice steady.

"Don't know," Mitchell said, and then he and his friends laughed like it was the best joke ever. They slung their own bags over their shoulders and ran off.

Brody didn't know what he would tell his Mum about his bag. His knees hurt as well, and he had stopped on the walk home to sit behind a tree and cry again. It hadn't helped much.

He was about a block from his house when he saw the possum. Or he was pretty sure it was a possum. It lay with its back legs and tail on the sidewalk but its head off in the dirt and leaves near the road. It was dead. Brody thought it must have been hit by a car until he got close, and then he knew that wasn't what happened. It was shrunken down, collapsed in on itself like the bird had been. Its eyes were open but sunken and glazed over. Its tongue hung out of its mouth, looking like a tiny flat piece of dry leather. There was a circle of dried bloodspots on its belly.

Brody gave it a poke with his shoe and it moved easily, like it was too light. It was stiff, too, like it was really old and all dried out, but it hadn't been there on his walk to school that morning.

There was a kind of mewling sound, and when Brody turned around he saw the orange cat not far down the sidewalk behind him. He could still see the knobs of its backbone, and now he could see its ribs, too. But worse than that, its belly was way too large, swollen up like a soccer ball. It tottered toward him, and when it opened its mouth to mewl again he saw the leeches there, now long and thick and wriggling as if excited. They stretched out towards him, as if they knew he was there.

Brody turned and ran the rest of the way home.

His dad got home just after bedtime and came in to say good-night. Brody started crying.

"I hate it here," he sobbed, his face in his pillow. "Why can't we go home?"

His dad rubbed his back for a bit without saying anything. When Brody sniffled and turned over, he saw his dad looked even more tired than his mum, and almost as sad as he felt himself.

"Is it school?" Dad asked.

Brody almost told him then, about Mitchell and his friends, even about the cat and the leeches. But one was tattling and the other sounded made up, so instead he shook his head.

"It's everything."

"I'm sorry, buddy," his dad said quietly. "We have to be here. There's nothing I can do about it. It will get better, better for all of us. It will."

His dad said that last bit kind of quiet, like he wasn't really talking to Brody, and then he just sat there for a bit, staring out the window. Brody wondered if he saw a sick looking orange cat out there in the moonlight, waddling around with a big round belly. But when he spoke again, it wasn't to say there was anything outside.

"It will get better, if you promise me you'll try and make it better for yourself. That can be hard, really hard, but you need to try. Can you do that?"

"Okay," Brody said, because there was nothing else to say. He had no idea how he could try and make things better, and things were already hard. He rolled towards the window and tried not to look for the cat.

Brody told his mother he had forgot his bag at school. She had sighed but not really said anything about it, just put his sandwich and a couple of snacks in his purple plastic lunchbox from when he was little. He had taken it without arguing and set off early enough that if he found his bag, he could put the baby lunchbox away in it before anyone saw. Before Mitchell saw.

That didn't make him feel better. He felt sick as he walked. He had promised his dad he would try to make things better but he didn't know how. His knees hurt, and when he touched it, the back of his head still hurt, too.

The dead possum was still where he had seen it, dry and deflated and sad. He rounded the next corner and there, in the middle of the sidewalk, was the cat. It lay on its side, unmoving. Its belly was distended, pink skin stretched like a balloon underneath the ginger fur. The rest of it was very thin, and it stared blankly ahead. It was dead.

Brody crouched down next to it. Its mouth was open, and the leeches lay flat and tangled around each other. He went and found a stick and came back and gave them a bit of a poke. When he did, they stirred and turned and began to wriggle, first slowly, and then faster. They twisted toward him, like they had before, as if they knew he was there, sensing he was near. They stretched out, and their tops opened, red and wet.

And then they pulled themselves free of the cat's mouth, sliding out of black holes where teeth should have been. First one, then two, then the rest. They wriggled down over the cat's dry tongue and onto the sidewalk and started towards Brody, curling and humping and moving very quickly.

Brody stood up and stepped back, and then stepped forward and ground his foot down. When he lifted it he saw he had crushed more than half of the leeches into the cement. Another step would get most of the rest. He felt a sudden sense of satisfaction. This was something only he knew about, but he was doing something to make it better. He stomped down again, getting most of the rest, grinding them into the cement and thinking of Mitchell. Thinking of his dad saying they had to be here, they didn't have a choice. That Brody needed to try and make things better.

Brody didn't say anything when Mitchell and his friends shoved him on the way into class. He had taken care of the leeches, and he would take care of this.

When Mitchell went to the toilet block near the end of lunch, he followed. He slipped into the next cubicle and crouched down on his hands and knees. There was plenty of space under the cubicle wall, enough space that Brody could crawl right on through if he wanted to. And Mitchell's feet were right there.

Now the time had come his stomach felt tight as well as empty. He almost got up and left, but he had promised his dad he would try to make things better. And his dad had said making things better might be hard.

He opened his lunchbox. It was almost empty. His sandwich and snacks lay next to the dead cat on the sidewalk. The leech inside raised itself up, moving this way and that, the red end opening up like the little mouth it was.

"Want some food?" Brody mouthed, like he had asked the cat under the house, and slid the box under the cubicle wall.

Dead-Go

The woman in front of me has the pale face and sunken eyes of the recently deceased. The real clincher, though, is the Dead-Go implant, shining like a flat black bug nestled in the stubble at the back of her head. She raises one hand and scratches at it, and then gives me a polite smile as her partner helps her further along the row of seats. She still has a ways to go to get all the way back, but she *is* back. Second chance city, baby.

Maybe it is bad taste to bring a dead person to something like this, but I'm not in a position to judge. At least they fill a couple more seats. Not many bother coming to a pre-funeral. They are confusing events, to put it mildly.

Herb's widow stops next to me.

"Hello," she says. Not a question, but a question all the same. You can't not answer a widow at her husband's own show. I stand up.

"Hello," I say, and take her hand as briefly as I can. I hate my job.

"I work with Herb," I say.

She smiles. She has been crying, but you can tell nowadays when someone isn't quite convinced of their own loss. There is hope reflected both in her cracked smile and in her mostly intact mascara—a fragile belief that the flat black implant in the back of her husband's head will fix what was once unfixable. While Dead-Go doesn't work all the time, it is more reliable than any of the cheaper knock-offs. And Herb is a prime candidate, having been taken by a relatively minor heart issue that has been corrected since. No issues rebooting a system with a burnt out motherboard, so to speak.

"Oh, lovely of you to come. And I hope Herb gets the chance to thank you, as well."

Sure. Herb is really going to thank me.

"I'm so glad Dead-Go is part of the company's employee package. You know, Herb and I laughed about it, when we saw it in the contract. So funny."

"Yes," I say. "But it may not take."

"Oh, I know," she says, and the almost-dryness of her eyes creeps me out. She doesn't know anything she should know.

She sweeps on to greet the dead woman and her partner in front of me, and I try to ignore her little laugh in response to something one of them says. She is expecting Herb to sit up shortly, and this little pre-funeral will become a welcome back party. Man, I *really* hate my job.

At least we don't have to sit through anything like a funeral or eulogy. That would be just too bizarre. There is an uncomfortable moment as everyone settles and then stares at the low, white-sheeted bed at the front of the initialisation room. Herb's widow stands up and glances at the Dead-Go technician in their almost clergy-like black suit. The technician nods and Herb's widow pushes the button on the sleek metallic stand next to the bed. For a second, nothing happens.

And then Herb sits up. No fanfare, no flashing lights or electronic buzzing. His wife gasps a little, in either relief or surprise, and there is a stilted clapping from someone, but it dies almost before it has begun. Herb looks around, his eyes as bloodshot as they probably looked after a late night of checking accounts at work. He raises one hand dreamily and scratches at his Dead-Go implant.

I'm a chicken. I wait until almost everyone is gone, and until Herb's wife has drifted away to talk to the dead woman and her partner. Maybe she is organising a double date or something.

"Hi, Herb," I say, and then wait. He is fresh, so he is going to be a bit slow on the uptake. He looks me over a little blearily.

"I know you?" he asks. He sounds like he has just woken up

from a long, particularly hard nap.

"I work for your company's HR, at Head Office."

His wife appears next to me. I was hoping to get this done before she came back, but there is nothing for it now. I hand over the large manila envelope. Herb's hand floats up slowly towards it, but his wife intercepts.

"What is this?" she asks. She should be suspicious, but she is still riding the high of Dead-Go putting her life back together.

"It's your relocation package," I say.

"What?" Her smile is fading. She doesn't get it yet, but she is close.

"We are growing in the southwest, and we need someone to manage the new accounts. Herb is the best we have."

Herb frowns slowly while his wife laughs uncomfortably.

"The company offered a transfer last year. We said no. Our whole life is here."

I shrug. Here we go.

"It's not negotiable."

She stares at me, looking very much like her husband—like she is slowly waking up.

"Well, Herb has lots of experience. He won't have trouble getting another job."

"True. We value him very highly, but he is free to leave, of course. All company property will have to be returned, though." I pause, letting my gaze move to the top of Herb's head. "All of it."

Her eyes widen. Herb is frowning now as well. He is coming around pretty quickly—a good indication of his value to the company. I turn away as his wife starts yelling. I've heard it all before, of course. I catch myself scratching at the back of my head and force myself to stop. I hate my job so damn much, but it's not like I've really got a choice.

Trial By Fire

Even in the bathroom my eyes sting from the smoke, and I can taste ash in the back of my throat. The world burns, it seems, over and over. There are cries for action, and the talking heads still argue on the news, but most people just battle along, having numbly accepted that the new normal is just that little bit closer to hell. Numb is probably best, here at the end of so much.

I met Kat while I was working for the university paper. She had won another in what was apparently a string of accolades and awards, while I was just starting to figure out journalism was not for me. Too much of it was just trying to look interested as people talked about fires and climate and air pollution. Sometimes politics. But really, everyone just wanted to talk about themselves. Talk, talk, talk.

"So, tell me about your research," I said as I looked for a pencil in my bag. She looked amused at my lack of organisation.

"I can't save the world," Kat replied.

"What?" I asked, pausing in my rummaging. She smiled at my confusion, all dark eyes and dimples.

"But I'm going to save some of it."

"Oh. Okay. And you are," I paused again, checking my notes, "an ecological futurist. What's that?"

"I work with genetics of ecological systems. I examine how they might evolve. How they might be encouraged to change in response to problems."

"What sort of problems? Like the fires? All the extinctions?"

"Exactly," Kat nodded, and her smile faded. "We've lost so much. So many species gone forever. Imagine, though, if we could tweak DNA to make organisms more resilient. Think of the species we could save."

"Like what we do with genetically modified food?"

Her dimples disappeared completely. "Please," she said, and for some reason I felt my face warm. "I'm not talking about viral carriers to ram pesticide resistance into a tomato. We would need something much more elegant, and certainly much more stable than that. I'm talking about splicing resilience into our most beloved, most endangered species."

"That sounds…dangerous," I said. I didn't want to say it. I thought maybe that might stop the dimples coming back, but it was out before I could stop myself.

She cocked her head slightly. "It's all theoretical, of course. Most people think we are a few years away from appropriate methods, let alone trials."

"Ah," I said. Just more talk, really. I felt oddly disappointed.

"Most people think that. I think we need to actually do something."

"Yes!" I said, killing off any semblance of professionalism I had with just one word. She looked at me curiously as I cleared my throat.

"Um… You've been awarded a highly competitive grant to further your research. Would you tell me more about that?"

"Maybe," she said after a slight pause, her head still cocked to one side…"over a drink?"

My article did well, and garnered a bit of follow-up. I had lost my taste for reporting, but I think my not-quite-professional interest in the subject had, in this one instance, lifted my bland, workaday writing into the realm of readability. Even as we went from our first drink to our first movie, and then took our first tentative steps beyond, Kat found herself interviewed on one sciencey podcast, and then another, one with a much larger audience. After that came a few old-style radio interviews, and then an appearance on a YouTube channel that specialised in cutting complex issues down to match the attention span of its several million subscribers.

It was the worst thing that could have happened.

"My analysis time has been reassigned!" she snapped one night as we sat on my sagging couch. "By accident, of course." The sarcasm in her voice was something new, something I didn't like. This was the latest in an ongoing pattern of subtle to not-so-subtle aggression from the upper storeys of academia's ivory tower. Woe unto those who attempt to climb too fast, and all that.

"The lab manager suggested I could maybe do some more interviews while I waited for the equipment to become available again. Or I could do my work in the middle of the night."

I could see the hollows under her eyes, the pale thinness of her face. I did not know what to say, so I sat and stared at the television, at the coverage of yet another fire. Smouldering, charred trees. Ash-covered slopes. A lump of something that might have been alive once, now blackened and twisted. As I watched, the lump shifted and moved, patches of fur breaking open into red wounds, a white eye rolling in anguish. Then the image fuzzed out and returned, mercifully grainy and pixelated. The local network was trying to broadcast through yet another record layer of smoke. The world just kept on burning, and I wondered if the sourness I tasted was smoke that my apartment's crappy filtration system couldn't handle, or just my own guilt. I had written that first article, after all.

"Kat, what is this really about? You're no newbie to this sort of thing. You were dealing with it well before we even met."

Kat bit her lip in hesitation for a moment, and then she replied, her voice high and wavering as she gestured at the dying creature on the screen. "God, look! Look at that! And I'm not *doing* anything! None of us are." Her voice twisted on this last, and I heard a new bitterness there, hard and sharp.

"So do something differently," I said. She looked startled. "I mean, remember what you said to me?"

She frowned.

"You're not going to save the world," I reminded her. "But

maybe you can still save some of it." Like her, I was sick of talk, yes, but I think I was really just responding to that bitterness in her voice. I wanted her to find her way back to her passion. And maybe to stop looking at whatever was dying on the television screen.

"What are you doing?" I asked a few nights later, while we were watching footage of yellow-suited fire fighters on some new and smouldering frontline of horror. Kat had been quiet since her last frustrated venting, and I had been trying to ignore a small fluttering of both worry and guilt. But now at least she was working on something, with just one eye on the news. More of the same there, of course. Skeletal, blackened trees. A smoking, twisted fire truck. Burnt, panting and pained wildlife. That was usually her real trigger, but tonight she had barely raised her head. She was bent over a notepad, sketching and muttering to herself. I had tried to peek, but it was the usual—equations, weird symbols, what looked like squares of numbers and letters. One I knew, because Kat sketched them up for absolutely everything—a Venn Diagram. *Bam.* Watch out, science, here I come. I was grinning to myself as Kat grabbed her tablet and turned to me. The image on the screen made my smile fade: a dead, blackened tree, with tiny green leaves sprouting straight from the trunk.

"This is epicormic growth," she said. "Heard of it?"

I shook my head. "But I've seen it," I said.

She nodded. "It's an evolutionary trait of eucalypts, other Myrtaceaes, and some other plant families. It's a last-ditch recovery effort after fire. They tap into their final reserves, try to recover. The final desperate sprint away from death."

"Okay," I said, not knowing where she was going. I rarely did, when she revved up.

She turned her notebook to me and tapped some equations. "Here. This is the gene sequence for the fastest epicormic growth response I can find. Mere hours to full bloom. What if we took that"—here she pointed at a long sequence of numbers and letters—"and inserted it here."

"Kat..." I began, but she was too far gone.

"This is a mock-up of the backbone sequencing for marsupials. Of course it's quite generic, but I can splice here"—she pointed at one spot—"and I think it should take in most species. Rapid regeneration. It's really quite simple." She paused, frowning. She tapped the Venn Diagram.

"But I have to work on this gene transfer and barrier concept. We can't have it bleeding out."

Bleeding out. I didn't like the sound of that, but Kat was already far away, trekking through the strange internal landscape of her own thoughts. I think I had disappeared by then, morphing into nothing more than a blank face she could talk at. Mostly her science speak just washed over me, but I hadn't been with her for so long without picking up a few things.

"Kat, you want to splice eucalypt genes into marsupials? Plants and vertebrates? Isn't that a big no-no? Even according to you?"

Kat glanced up at me, her pencil in her mouth. "Hmmmm?" she said absently. I stared at her, and she finally focused on me as my words bounced around in her head. When she did, I saw some of that new bitterness, that new anger there in her expression. Hell, I saw a lot of it.

"We have to do something," she said, and pointed at the damn television. "*I* have to. I've wasted too much time already."

I didn't say anything, but I couldn't stop staring at that Venn Diagram.

It took months. Days, nights, weekends. I don't know how much of that time was spent circumnavigating colleagues and procedures, and how much of it was just the plain old difficulty of cutting-edge science, but she would appear only at irregular intervals, eating quickly, catching a nap, showering occasionally. She began to lose weight. Her eyes grew even larger and darker in her thin face, and she developed a habit of chewing hard on her lower lip, but she would smile a real smile when I pushed another sandwich at her, or when I dropped in a change of clothes after hours at the lab. By the end she was on the verge of emaciation, and her forehead was lined with deep frown marks, but that sour twist to her lips and that bitterness in her voice were gone. And God help me, I was complicit the whole time. Not because I wanted to save the world from burning, or even just a few animals. I just wanted that bitterness in her face to go away, for that hard note in her voice to disappear.

I didn't know how she released it, or how she made it so effective so fast, and I doubt I would've understood if she told me. But it wasn't long until the nightly fire report deviated to footage of the first marvel—healthy pink skin growing on a Koala's ravaged back just a day after it had sustained third-degree burns. Halfway through the rambling commentary, Kat sighed and curled up next to me on the couch, falling into a sleep so deep I put my hand on her chest lightly to feel her breathing.

The next day a friend sent me a TikTok of wallabies standing healthy and hale on smoking ground, fine fur already growing over new, baby-fresh skin. The damn thing was set to Leonard Cohen's Hallelujah, which made me groan. I didn't show Kat that one, but I did show her the next—an echidna waddling across my tablet screen, tiny spikes jutting up on its back, fresh and new like small brown shoots. Mere hours later it had waddled across a few million other screens as it went properly viral. Kat actually clapped her hands when she saw it, and then squealed and hugged me tight.

"It took you to remind me," she said, beaming. "Maybe I can't save the world, but I can save some of it."

"Will you tell everyone?" I asked, as Kat packed her bag. She had been asked to join a panel of experts convening to discuss the spontaneous marsupial regeneration phenomenon, as it was being called in scientific circles. Everyone else was calling it a miracle, but trust scientists to go the stodgy route.

"I don't know," she said as she folded her jeans.

"You would get in trouble," I said, pretty pointlessly.

"I wouldn't have done it if I cared about that," she replied, shrugging. "But someone will find the splicing, and the viral carrier I used, once they start looking properly."

"Viral carrier?" I echoed. That was the first I'd heard about that. "I thought you said your work would need something more stable than that."

"Yes," Kat said. "And I also said we were years away from that. I needed something that would work *now*. And would spread quickly."

She said it so matter-of-factly, I did not know what to say in response. I watched her finish packing in silence, but I couldn't stop thinking about that damn Venn Diagram.

Kat had been gone for less than two days when the wash of images and videos changed, flickering and wavering with all the smoke in the air, but still all too clear. That first miracle koala had been put into isolation while its new skin bubbled and blistered, pushing up from its back in long, purplish tendrils of bumpy, gnarled flesh. Some sort of dark liquid oozed out as the delightfully horrified reporter breathlessly described what she couldn't understand.

Next came a park ranger, her face stark as she described three kangaroos lying by a fire trail. They had huge, twisting growths pushing out from their abdomens, making them scrabble and fall as they tried to move. Then came other reports, other rumours. Photos from firefighters on the television, and Facebook feeds from wannabe citizen journalists. First it was just marsupials, and only those that had been burnt. Then it wasn't just them, and it wasn't just the injured. Sheep, cattle. People's pets. It was spreading, well, like wildfire.

It just kept on coming, scene after scene, all different, all the same, all horrific. I stared as a news anchor appeared on the screen, warning everyone, yet again, that the upcoming footage was of a sensitive nature. The image switched to a horse in a field, its screaming almost human as it thrashed and tried to drag itself along, huge purple tendrils hanging from its hindquarters.

I turned away at that, trying not to hear those screams. Trying not to see those writhing tendrils. Trying not to think of epicormic growth of burnt eucalypts, of charred flesh and viral carriers and gene transfer barriers. Trying not to picture that damn Venn Diagram.

Kat stood in the doorway, her face white, her eyes fixed on the screen.

"It's bleeding out," she whispered.

Yes, I wish I were numb, here at the end.

"Can we go?" Kat calls from the other side of the bathroom door, her voice high and glassy. I don't reply. We are heading out to talk to the university, and then, no doubt, the media. She is holding herself together, but only just. It will be the end of everything for her, but she thinks she knows how it will go. She has even talked about still trying to fix it, if she can get others to help.

I'm thinking any fix might be too late. I look down at my arm again. The growths have come on fast. They were just itchy lumps an hour ago, but now they protrude upward, purplish and angry and weeping. They seem to lengthen even as I watch, but surely that is just my imagination.

I close my eyes, and all I can see is fire, and smoke, and that damn Venn Diagram.

Bleeding out, I hear Kat whisper. It seems so very apt.

A Tomorrow With You In It

It is dark when they come, banging on the door so loudly that I know they are bringing death with them. I hurry to answer it. I can see you stir in the sleeping alcove, little more than a hump under the blankets, but you are tired out from a day of laughing and climbing and tugging on my skirt, and you do not wake.

The night sounds of the city flow in as I open the door. Hawkers from the late market call and plead over the rise and fall of revellers from a nearby tavern. There is a distant crashing, and then a scream followed by hoarse laughter. Sounds of life, and choice, and chance.

Two men stand on my threshold. One, Iyaan, I know from the market, where he sells the sugared plums you are so greedy for. He has dark hair shot through with grey, and stubble that is more salt than pepper. City life has left its mark on him, but he has kind eyes and an engaging grin. Now, he is serious and pale.

The other is younger. Little more than a man, but he looks as a child with the fear writ large on his face. His eyes are wide, the whites showing all around, and he has been crying. No, he *is* crying. I start to close the door.

"Please," he says. "Please." He holds out the limp form in his arms, and I curse inwardly. The little girl looks like she is asleep, but she is not. I know that by the way she lays, boneless and still like a broken bird.

I told myself I would not, not again, but she seems so like you. She has the same soft curls, and there is something to the slight upturn of her nose. I am sure it crinkles when she cries. When she cried. Before I can stop myself, I reach out. Her skin is soft and cool and her face is calm, but I can see small scarlet droplets in her long eyelashes, and in those dark curls. I feel the tomorrows rent and torn. Here, a flash of dancing in red shoes, giggling with delight. Here, a possible journey, the taste of dust and adventure on parched lips. And here, the bitterness of a first broken heart. The possibilities flail, greying and growing sluggish even as I sense them. My gaze is drawn to you, and then back to this broken creature.

"What happened?" I ask softly.

"She—" The younger man hitches his breath, fights the tears, and then tries again. "She fell. Down the steps. Our home, it is on the west wall."

Simple enough. Such a mundane accident is common enough, too, if you live in one of the city wall slums, rickety buildings that sit atop one another like chipped and uneven stones. The city is full of danger. This you will learn.

"She is dead," I say. I hear the flatness of my own voice, and I hate it. But some things need to be said, before what comes next.

"What would you have of me?"

Both men look uncomfortable in their own ways, and I suppress a sigh. You will find that most people cannot give voice to the impossible, no matter how much they want it.

It has been long, and longer, since I have been asked to do this. There was a time when such as I, such as we, were more common, but we are not built to last. Chance and choice take us early if we persist. I do not want to do it—I hope you believe that. But she is so like you. And she would have had red shoes, or an adventure, or heartache. Or so many other tomorrows.

"Put her on the rug," I say. You have not wakened, and I doubt you will. You sleep the deepest of sleeps, as I did as a child before you. Time enough for sleeplessness when you are older, when you give away the tomorrows that you have. Oh, my love, please have more care than I.

The younger man lays the girl down in the middle of our small living space, and I motion for him to step back. What I am to do is both simple and the hardest thing. I glance to you again, but not to check your sleep. I should not do this thing, should not risk what I risk, but she has those curls, and had those tomorrows. How can I turn away those that have come? Am I so selfish as to risk nothing?

"You must promise," I say, turning to hold my visitors with my eyes.

"Anything!" the young man sobs, and Iyaan nods quickly.

"Two things," I continue, without acknowledging their hastiness. "First, you must not tell others." Here, I fix Iyaan with a cold eye and he has the grace to blush. It makes him more than handsome. I can see the remnants of the child he was, before the city marked him with its weight. My heart twists a little.

"Second," I continue, "if something happens to me, tomorrow or the next day or maybe months from now, you must promise to care for mine, if no one else makes a claim you think is just." It has been long since I have done this thing, and extracted such a promise. I do not know if my last visitors would still consider themselves bound, as belief in strange things dwindles so with time. But Iyaan has those kind eyes, and his friend cries so for his lost daughter. They are both good things to see, so I ask.

There is a moment of silence as they digest my words. Iyaan's eyes widen, and he makes as if to speak. I raise one hand to stop him. I look at the younger man, the girl's father, and I see what I need there on his face: hope, and pain, and perhaps the small beginnings of understanding.

I kneel by the girl. I do not search for her injuries. They are not important. I do not know where this gift, or this curse, or both, comes from. I know it was in my mother, and I feel it in your small, chubby hands as they grasp mine. It is much the same as I feel from others, twisting threads of chance, but in yours, I feel this curse, this skill, this risk, winding its way through your days.

In the girl, the threads are torn and fading. I see again the red shoes, taste the dust and thirst, feel the heartache. And more besides, but now they are all like whispers, sun-faded paintings, echoes. I turn to regard the men. Their pathways are strong, bright and silver. The girl's father has but a handful left to him, even at his young age. In one, he is destitute, bereft, a failure. In several others, he dies early, but not completely unhappy. There are a few wavering, silvery threads of hope still there, hovering about him, stretching up and away to a future that may grow from a miracle.

Iyaan is different. His pathways are few, and gleam with solid chances of becoming. I am a little surprised to see one silvery line flash with an image of me, bright and twisting with emotion. With an effort, I put my desire to trace it, to see what I can see, aside. You must do the same, when fate tempts you. You will never see enough, and the taste of those bright threads of chance are so very bitter.

I look back to the girl. I know what she would have had, if I had seen her earlier. Silvery threads of possible futures spilling out of her, splitting, merging, twisting and branching, choices made and ignored, her many lives flickering as possibilities. Now, there are just those fading threads, the last flickers of a fire that has burnt to embers.

I reach up to my own threads. There are not that many of them, and I do not see them as clearly as I see others. I let my fingers brush one, then another. There is an art to what I do, to what you may feel compelled to do. You need one that will take root, but you must select so very carefully. The first I touch has the smell of flatbread and long, warm summer days, the ache of old bones. It fills me with both satisfaction and tiredness. It is not of interest to a young girl on the edge of life. The second is nothing but tears and hollowness, and I push it away from me. The third—there is a flash of laughter and childish spirits. I draw in a sharp breath as I see you, smiling and spinning, watching your dress twirl in the late afternoon sun. You are older, but not much, and I feel an ache inside as I close my hand around the thread. It will work.

I pluck the thread even as my eyes well with tears. I have not changed the chance you will spin and smile—I cannot do that. But if that future firms and grows, I will not see it.

I give the thread to the girl. She is young, and there was at least a possibility before this that she would one day dance and giggle in red shoes. It is enough. The thread catches and holds and shimmers. It will grow and split and spread, choices wending their way back into her tomorrows. The rootstock is strong and well-matched.

The girl breathes deeply and her father cries out. I slump back on my haunches and wave at them to leave me be. I am not tired, but I ache inside. The image of you spinning and smiling is fading, and I feel…I don't know. Less. Ashamed. I should be able to say no. I cannot say no. I do not understand myself, and yet I hope one day you will.

Iyaan hustles the man and his daughter away, shushing them both as they cry, him in relief, her in confusion. He whispers to me he shall return to see me later, but I do not want to look for that thread that may run from him to me. It was the future, and it was only a chance anyway.

My tea cools in my hand as I sit by the window, listening to the city, listening to the choices being made, the futures winnowed from silvery chance. I order my thoughts as best I can, but it is hard. Soon, I will write the story of tonight, and hope you will one day hear it from my lips, rather than read it on old, dry parchment.

What I do is what I must, but I don't know if I can keep on, or if I should. I close my eyes and see a young girl, dancing in red shoes. I try to see you, spinning in the afternoon sun, and I cannot. It is nothing but the memory of a day I will never see. The memory of a tomorrow with you in it.

Renting Space

The room is dim, but not really dark. The sun has not quite gone down yet, and I can see it through the front window, large and orange and seeming to bulge as it sinks behind the buildings across the street. There is enough of that baleful, feverish light to just read what I am writing. It is so quiet I can hear my pencil scratching across the paper.

I know what people say about real estate agents. It's no big secret. Pushy. Disingenuous. But I can tell you, it's a cut-throat business. I'm new to it, and I've got to say, it's the very first thing you learn. Those wide, fake smiles turn into maniacal grins when you are back in the office. The air smells of desperation and sweat.

But I'm sitting here now to say, flat out, I would never do something that would get someone killed. I'm writing it down. I want it all documented. And I'm going to find out the truth. At least I'll know. That will be something.

Like I said, I'm new to the business, and to be honest, I'm not passionate about it. It's not my calling. I suppose that's my problem. I'm not passionate about anything, really. My father used to say that a lot. But I don't want to spend time going over my background. One, it's boring. Two, it's getting darker, and I don't want to switch the light on. That will make sense to you in a bit, I guess.

Suffice to say my story is short and clichéd. My school career was sad and hollow, an exercise in treading water in a pool I couldn't find the edge of. Despite that, I found myself finishing high school both successfully (just), and with a girlfriend who I loved, and who I was sure loved me back. We would beat this nasty, unfair world together. Cue the power ballad.

She went to university. I had no desire to swim from a shallow pool of learning out into the middle of an ocean, so I followed but mooched around, holding down a handful of low paying, zero reward positions. If you had asked me what I was about, and what my goals were, I wouldn't have been able to answer. I guess I still can't answer that, although right now, I'd say I want answers. That more than anything.

I handed out flyers. I delivered pizzas. I even washed cars. I saw less of my soulmate than I did of sweaty kitchens and print shops, and even when I made it home early enough, she never seemed to be there. The writing on the wall couldn't have been in larger print, but I was still floored when she left me. Or demanded I leave her, and her apartment. She wasn't even upset. She just had a kind of relief on her face that I couldn't argue with. I won't dwell on it. It is boring, and oh-so typical, but it also hurts, a lot.

I couldn't go home. My parents would take me in, but I knew I had seen a version of that same relief on their faces when I'd said adios to them not so long ago. That hurt too, but I suppose I couldn't really blame them. I was a bit of a space-filler. So I did what I always did, and I went on autopilot. I tried not to think of anything, and I doubled down on work. I moved out, taking over a lease on a tiny studio apartment from a thin, pale girl who seemed two steps down the road from where I was. She left literally dragging her belongings in a bag behind her. Watching her go scared me. I went to work with a hollow sort of gusto. I delivered food. I swept floors. I even caught some shifts at the recycling centre, sorting paper and plastic. Some nights I fell asleep stinking of fried rice and mouldy paper. I was the hardest working slacker in existence, but I was still going broke.

I cast about for something in my desperation, but I kept coming up empty. The months just after university started for the year was a dismal time to be searching for unqualified work in a university town. I could afford—barely—to work and live with a frugal and loving partner who would quietly bear most of the burden, but on my own, I was quickly drowning.

Finally, after a breakfast of cold, undelivered pizza and a rummage for a rumpled t-shirt that smelt more like Chinese food than garbage, I went in to try and explain the situation to my real estate agent. The place where I was living was little more than a closet, but I couldn't afford it. God knew what I thought I was going to do. I couldn't break my lease. I couldn't pay my rent. If the receptionist hadn't been at lunch, I probably would've been out on my ear in thirty seconds. But the desk was empty, and I stood there, unsure of what to do. I guess I was hoping for the hand of God, and in a weird way, I got it. The hand of Thompson.

"She's out at lunch," a reedy voice said.

I started and looked up. A head was poking around the corner of the hallway behind the receptionist's desk. A big, bald, shockingly white head. It looked huge, actually, because his features were all crowded in the middle of his smooth face. Little pug nose, beady eyes, thin lips. Huge, bushy eyebrows. One of those faces that leave you increasingly bewildered, the more you look at it, as you wonder how such a configuration of features could exist. But he was smiling slightly, and even as I stared at him, he slipped around the corner and stepped toward me. He was dressed in a grey suit with a light blue tie. He was thin enough that his head looked unsteady and massively out of proportion. He leant on the receptionist's desk, and I swear, his eyes seemed to twinkle a little.

"Let me guess," he said, his voice light and oddly sing-song. "Rent problems?"

I nodded. I had no idea what to say. I was suddenly very aware of the smell of sweet and sour pork rising up from my shirt.

He tapped the desk for a moment. His eyes were friendly and thoughtful.

"You know," he said finally. "I've seen you before." He raised one hand. "Not here. I saw you driving the pizza delivery car from Romero's. Yes?"

I nodded, and he nodded in turn. It was like watching one of those drinking bird ornaments with the bulbous, bobbing heads. Mesmerising.

"And handing out fliers for the coffee shop?"

I nodded again. He nodded again. We both nodded, again.

"How many jobs do you have?" he asked, and I shrugged. Adding them all up, they were still less than one. I said so, and he laughed.

There was a bell over the door, one of the little, old fashioned silver jobs that tinkled when the door opened. It did its thing now, and I turned around to see the receptionist. Her face clouded slightly when she saw me. It wasn't the first time I'd been late on the rent. But then her gaze drifted beyond me and she smiled, professional and fake and devoid of all real emotion.

"Mr Thompson!" she said, stepping forward quickly. "I can take care of this."

But he waved the idea away with one hand and then pointed to the corridor with the other. "No need. I'd actually like to chat with…" He looked pointedly at me, and after a moment I realised he was waiting for my name.

"Jim," I supplied. He nodded, and before I knew it, I was being ushered down the corridor.

But what am I doing? I said I needed to hurry, and you don't need to know all this. Summarise, summarise, that's what I should be doing. I'm squinting at the paper in front of me as I go. I might need to turn the light on. I know the power is still on, but I don't want anyone looking in and seeing the light. I'd rather just finish.

Jerry Thompson owned the real estate agency. He seemed nice at first. I couldn't smell the sweat and desperation in his office. I guess it was too far from the bull pen, where the three more junior staff worked at both sales and rentals. Sales brought in the bucks. Rentals gave the constant trickle of cash that made the banks happy with an otherwise wildly fluctuating bottom line. That's what Mr Thompson said.

He said other things, too, while we sat in his sterile office and I watched his giant head bob up and down, but it all boiled down to one thing. He was short a person. He wouldn't lie. Staff turnover in the business was high, but the job could be good for someone who worked hard. He couldn't pay me much, but the figure he trotted out seemed astronomical to me. Trial basis, and I'd have to do some real estate course to get accredited, and he'd drop me like a sack of something unpleasant if I didn't stack up. And what did I think about it all?

I said yes. Of course I did. What choice did I really have? I suppose I could've gone home, but like I said, that wasn't very appealing. The offer really seemed a godsend. We shook on it, I filled out a bunch of paperwork, and I got an advance. I bought a cheap suit and turned up early the next day. It took two weeks for me to stop smelling Chinese food and pizza every time I breathed deeply. I don't know if that was real or just in my mind, but I wasn't game to ask anyone about it.

And I was really too anxious to dwell on body odour. I guess I should've questioned the whole thing. I mean, who hires someone like that? The other staff did not bat an eyelid when Mr Thompson introduced me around the next morning. They smiled and nodded and said the pleasant things you say when your boss is watching you interact with someone. A slightly puffy woman named Julie in a too-tight pantsuit gave me two huge binders, smiling a bit too widely as she did so. One was for studying—it was full of rules and procedures and frequently asked questions. It was also very well laid out, and now that I think of it, very well thumbed. I wonder how many versions of me had been through that office.

The second binder was actually where the trouble started. Started and I guess finished, as well. The binder listed our current rentals, and that was where I was to start.

Julie sat next to me as I browsed our collection. She was still smiling too widely. Her eyebrows were plucked so razor thin it looked like she had creases above her eyes.

"It's a bad time to start," she said morosely, and it took me a moment to register the meaning of what she said against her bonkers cheerful demeanour. She wouldn't stop smiling. Her teeth were very white. Over the next few weeks I would find myself, more and more, smiling that same smile. It just kind of permeated throughout the office. Smiling at clients. Smiling at Mr Thompson. Smiling insanely at the other people in the office. I would go to sleep with my face hurting from it.

"What do you mean?" I asked.

She shrugged, still smiling, but her eyes seemed almost blank, like she'd been through this routine before and was just trotting it all out once again.

"The students are all here. Best time to fill rentals was three months ago. But we need to drop our vacancies. Too high."

"What do I need to do?" I asked, and she shrugged.

"One a week."

"Fill one vacancy a week?" I asked. It didn't seem that hard. She kept smiling as she stood up, but her eyes had already drifted away. She brushed some imaginary creases from the front of her suit. I don't know why she bothered. It was so tight there was no way a wrinkle could worm its way into the fabric.

I couldn't do it. Looking back, it was absurd. Not the task itself, but me being in the position. I guess Thompson's approach was the shit-to-the-wall type of management. You know what I mean: throw it, see what sticks. In this case, the shit was me, and I'm pretty sure I wasn't going to be the sticking type.

I felt useless from the outset. I kept thinking of a documentary I had seen when I was a kid. It was about a spider that sat and waited for prey to come close enough for it to grab. At the time it had seemed kind of cool, a minimal effort kind of evolution. But as I sat with that binder in my stupid grey cubicle I wondered how long a spider like that could last in a world devoid of prey. The days ticked by. Smiles abounded. People were busy, talking on phones, showing clients around, even making sales, but hardly anyone seemed to be interested in rentals. I showed a few properties to dull-eyed browsers. As the days turned first into one week, and then two, Mr Thompson was not smiling any more. Not at me, anyway.

"You've got to fill some vacancies," he said, after he'd called me into his office. He looked concerned, but it was a shallow look that didn't reach his eyes.

"Mr Thompson," I replied, "I don't know what to do. No one is coming in. No one is calling."

He smiled then, but it looked different. Tighter. Firmer. Suddenly his large head and small features did not look so comical. His small eyes didn't twinkle. They had gone flat.

"Ah," he said, nodding slightly. "So you thought you just needed to sit and wait."

I did not know if it was a statement or a question. I stayed silent. He fell silent. We were silent together.

Finally he made a little huffing sound. "I told you this was a good job for someone who would work hard. You seemed like you were a hard worker. Was I wrong?"

I shook my head, but inside, I wondered. Maybe I wasn't doing enough. Maybe I didn't want to. I thought of my girlfriend, and it hurt. What else did I have?

"Julie says it's a bad time to start." I tried to call back the words even as I said them, but it was too late. Mr Thompson was definitely not smiling now. He stared at me hard, and then raised one finger.

"Fill a vacancy. You have until the end of the week." And then he smiled widely. "You can do it, Jim."

I stood to leave.

"Oh," he continued. "Send Julie in, would you?"

Julie still smiled at me after that, but it looked like she had bitten into a rotten pear when she did it. I didn't mind much. I figured I probably wouldn't be there much longer to be smiled at, anyway.

I spent the afternoon staring at my binder of vacancies. It had way too many pages in it, but that didn't even seem to matter. Hardly anyone was looking. I sat there as the office slowly quieted around me. Eventually I was just sitting there alone, avoiding going back to my cupboard of a flat, when I heard the little bell over the door tinkle, bright and silvery.

I have to stop writing for a minute. That thick orange light from the sinking sun has been fading slowly, but now it is suddenly fading fast. I'm squinting at the page, trying to see what I am doing, and I realise I'm now surrounded by nothing but shadows.

I've turned the light on. I've looked back over the pages I've written, and I haven't even gotten to what I really need to say. I hope no one sees the light, but I'm going to risk it. I don't like it, and not just because I'm worried someone will see me in here. From here I can see the dark rectangle of the hallway. It is too hard to see anything out there now, against the light, but it is sitting like an open sore at the edge of my vision. I can hear the scratching of the pencil as I write, just like before, but I have to admit I am straining to hear something else.

Maybe I want to hear something.

Anyway, the bell tinkled, and I sighed and pushed myself away from my desk. I held the binder in one hand without noticing.

"We're closed," I said, even as I rounded the corner of the hallway and came into view of the empty reception desk.

A woman stood on the other side of the desk. She looked tired. Her hair was blonde, and a bit mussed by the day, and she wore a blouse and jeans ensemble that even I could probably afford. She smiled slightly and her eyes seemed to sink backwards into darkness. I was wrong. She wasn't tired. She was exhausted.

"Sorry," she said. "I couldn't get off work earlier."

We stared at each other for a moment, and then I remembered and plastered on my maniac smile. Hers faltered a little in response, which I understood completely. I probably looked like a serial killer. I probably looked like Julie.

"No problem," I said, and felt my cheeks ache as my smile grew a fraction wider. "What can I do for you?"

And of course she wanted to rent something. If this was a movie she would be cute, and our little transaction would save my job, and we would both be fulfilled somehow by meeting each other. But this wasn't a movie. She wasn't cute. She was much older than me, and kind of, well, just flattened out, trod upon by my old friend, reality. And here I stood, with the binder in my hand and the stink of desperation all around me, a smell that had replaced pizza and Chinese food, but was really just the same smell.

We leant on opposite sides of the receptionist's desk as I flipped the pages of the binder. She wasn't looking at the pages.

"I need it cheap. It's me and my daughter." She paused. I kept flipping pages. "She's fifteen." Like that was a nugget of information I really needed. I did nod my head, but that was the extent of my consideration. Crass. I could've done them the courtesy of spending more than one second considering their existence.

And then, page 12. "That one," she said, and stabbed a finger at the page. I looked up at her and she must've seen the question in my eyes. She shrugged.

"It's the cheapest I've seen. Two bedrooms. Close to my work. I'll take it." She paused, and then, her voice a little uncertain: "Yes?"

I'd read the other binder. It wasn't that simple. References, deposits, all that jazz. But then I thought of Mr Thompson, and the week I had to save my shitty closet of an apartment, not to mention my shitty job.

"Tomorrow morning. We can go and you can look at it. First thing."

She smiled. I smiled. Just a pair of happy people, getting things sorted out.

I pause in my writing again. A car has gone past outside. I saw the lights, and I was sure for a moment that it had slowed down. But it kept going, and I know deep down that I'm being paranoid. The police won't be interested. This is not a crime scene. I don't know what it is, not really.

But I want to find out.

Her name was Lucy. I met her at the house in the morning, early, before her work. I didn't mind. I mean, I was going to keep my job by doing this, at least for another week.

I'd be lying if I said I got a bad vibe from the place. There were only two things that were really noteworthy about it. The first was the painful 1970s décor. The kitchen had orange plastic benchtops and a green-and-orange diamond pattern that screamed up at you from the linoleum floor. The carpet was thick and a deep, deep blue, and the walls were faux chestnut panelling. *Yum.* The second thing was the price. It was almost alarmingly cheap, for a house. I mean, it was small, only two bedrooms, with that vintage porn interior and a yard so small you couldn't spin around in it, but still… It was super cheap. And it looked like we had had it listed for a long time.

I didn't even bother with a spiel. She walked through and turned the tap on in the kitchen, watching the water flow. She flushed the toilet. We both stood and listened to the small shuddering of water hammer in the walls, and she shrugged. I smiled my insane smile, and looked down at the extra pages of information I had. I frowned.

"Um, standard bond. First and last week rent in advance, and…" I paused, digesting what I had read. I looked at the ring of keys in my hand. Yep, there it was—an extra key with a number 3 engraved in spidery, amateurish script on the side.

"What?" she asked, and I could hear the worry in her voice. Desperation recognises itself, I guess. We were a pair, at least in that regard.

I frowned. "This says there is a third room, but it's not for rent." I flicked the page over and back again, but there was nothing else. "Um… It says storage." I looked at her. "The renter is not to have a key."

"Oh," she said, and then fell silent. She stared at me, and I stared at her. I suppose I should've said something, but I had no idea what that something should be. This was closer than I'd ever gotten to actually doing my job. I think I was more worried than she was that it might fall through.

"That feels a bit odd," she finally said. I nodded. She was right. We lapsed into silence again, giving us time to really feel the awkwardness of the whole situation.

"Can I at least look in there?" she asked. "I mean, I'd like to make sure it's not, like, I don't know, a torture chamber or a sweatshop or something."

"Well, I think you'd hear sewing machines if it was a sweatshop," I said, and then bit my lip.

She smiled slightly but said nothing. I wished she wouldn't smile. It made her look a thousand years old, all weary eyes and crushed struggle.

"Okay," I said. I didn't know if I should, but I had the key, so what the hell, right? And if it was something weird in there, at least I'd close out my illustrious career with a cool story.

I stop for just a moment, and I am a little freaked by the silence that flows in when I lean back in the chair. It scares me. Well, what I might hear in that silence scares me, I guess. Huh. A cool story. I wished I hadn't written that down. I wish I hadn't thought that.

The house had a kitchen and lounge room at the front, a long corridor, two bedrooms and a bathroom at the back. The third room was halfway along the corridor, hiding behind a heavy looking mahogany door. A dark red-brown, almost maroon door. There was a silvery knob, a solid looking modern lock plate and keyhole with the word *Yale* engraved in block letters across the front. Looking at it made me feel serious. Not afraid, just responsible. I had the key. I was going to open the door.

I glanced at Lucy. She was staring at the door.

"Ready?" I asked. I don't know why. She nodded and I slipped the key into the lock and turned. There was a smooth click, and I gave the door a little push. Nothing happened. I pushed harder, and it moved about an inch. I looked down. The carpet stopped at the doorframe, and I could see deep score marks where the door had scraped against the wood of the floor in the past. I shoved harder and there was a horrible sound of wood squealing against wood, almost like fingers down a chalkboard. I got it open just wide enough for us to slip in.

The room was empty. Completely empty. I mean, there wasn't

even that lovely blue carpeting, just dusty floorboards. There was a window that must've looked out on the neighbour's yard, but it had either been whitewashed a long time ago or was so filthy it made no difference. I breathed out, and as I did so, I heard Lucy do the same. We must have both been holding our breath. Looking back now, I guess the subconscious knows a lot more than the bumbling over-brain does.

"Why is it closed off?" she asked. I shrugged, although I knew what she meant. Storage? There was nothing stored in here but dust. There wasn't another answer I could give her. We stared around the room for a moment, and then she turned away. "Close it," she said, and walked towards the kitchen.

I closed it. It took some doing. I jerked on the handle repeatedly, moving the door about an inch each time. That squealing sound accompanied each tug as the door scraped across the wooden floor. Finally I got it closed, and I locked it. I know I did. I remember distinctly the feel and sound of the lock clicking back into place. I even remember giving the door a hard shove to be sure. It was locked solid.

Obviously she signed the lease. Paid the bond. Ticked the boxes. She wanted the place, and she could afford the place, and I needed the rental. The holy trifecta. I left her with the keys and hightailed it to work to deliver the astounding news that I didn't need to be fired for another week.

Mr Thompson's reaction was not what I would call ecstatic.

"You rented that place?" he asked when I told him. He looked pale. Julie was there too, and her wide and insane smile sagged into oblivion as I spoke. She looked like she had just discovered that I spent the evenings rubbing my crotch all over her desk or something. I ignored her, and confirmed for Mr Thompson that I had, indeed, done my job and rented one of the places in the binder.

"Ah," he said quietly.

"What's the matter?" I asked. I should have expected something. Just my luck.

Mr Thompson fell silent for a long moment. He looked pensive.

Finally he nodded to himself and looked up.

"Nothing for you to worry about. Just ancient history." He smiled, creeping me out. I shot a quick glance at Julie, who also attempted a wavering, toothy smile, maxing out my creep factor. He waved me away, and I went, lugging my misgivings with me. What the hell, I'd done my job.

One day. That was all it took. Or one night, rather, and then the cops called. Was I the rental agent? Could I go around? Lucy was almost hysterical. I could hear her in the background.

She pounced as soon as I walked in the open front door.

"Open that door!" she all but screamed in my face. I did a double take, even as a uniformed police officer gently inserted himself between us. Lucy stared at me, the shadows under her eyes a dark purple, her cheeks white, her eyes wide.

"What's happened?" I asked, looking around. I was on the edge of the kitchen. I could see several cardboard boxes sitting here and there. Two were open, and there were some plates and utensils stacked on one kitchen bench, the detritus from a weak effort at moving in. The police officer held me by the upper arm and steered me down the corridor. Lucy begrudgingly fell back before us. She glared at me. I could see clear snot on her upper lip. Her eyes were bloodshot.

"This woman's daughter is missing," the officer said. I stopped walking, and felt his fingers dig into my arm. He was short, and a bit pudgy, but his grip was strong.

"What?" I heard myself ask. Inane, but that's generally how humans react in a crisis, I guess.

"She's in there!" Lucy spat, and jerked one hand at the locked maroon door. We had already reached it. The house was small, and the corridor was not long.

"In there?" I repeated. "How?"

No one replied. I could hear the low murmur of voices from the kitchen. More police, talking quietly, calmly.

"Can you open it?" The first officer asked, and I nodded. I had the keys in my pocket, which was not a coincidence. A police officer had called me. I had brought everything to do with the property. I even had the binder under my arm.

Lucy stepped aside, giving me barely enough room to reach the door. I stuck the key in and turned it. The lock clicked, and Lucy pushed past me to shove hard on the door. Just like before, it gave grudgingly, making an ugly scraping sound against the floor. She got it open much wider than I had previously. The police officer stepped in behind her, and unsure of what I should do, I followed.

The room was empty. There was a faint layer of dust across the floorboards that Lucy had stirred as she entered. I could see individual dust motes floating in the dim morning light that was struggling through the dirty window.

Lucy visibly sagged. The police officer nodded to himself.

"But I heard it!" Lucy said. She turned to stare at me, her face haggard and eyes pleading.

The police officer stepped forward. He was pudgy, and short, like I said, but he had a kind face. "Tell me again," he said. He sounded very patient.

Lucy didn't look at him. She looked at me.

"Elizabeth. Betty. You never asked me her name."

I didn't know what to say. She was right, I hadn't asked. The police officer cleared his throat, and Lucy spoke again. She didn't look at him, though. She kept staring at me.

"She would never run away. Never."

"Ma'am," the officer said quietly. Lucy shook her head as if she could force his words away. She took a deep breath and cast her eyes around the room again, as if she couldn't believe the emptiness.

"We didn't get much unpacked. I had work, and Betty had school. But we got the beds in, and made some headway with the other boxes…" She fell silent, and then gave one wet sob. "This was supposed to be our time!"

I looked at the officer. He flicked his gaze to me and then back to Lucy. I couldn't tell what he was thinking. He had a bushy little moustache, and as I watched, he started sucking on it. I don't think he knew he was doing it.

Lucy had started speaking again. "We were both tired. We went to bed early." She looked at the officer, and I had the feeling this had been a thing between them.

"I heard it! I heard the click, and then the door opening." She flicked her gaze to me, and then back to the officer, and then back to me again. "I got up, and when I stepped into the corridor, I saw that door closing!" she thrust a trembling finger at the door behind us.

I didn't know what to say. The police officer said nothing, but he bent down and examined the bottom of the door. He reached out with one hand and lightly touched the scratch marks where the door had scraped across the wood. A few marks were fresh, but most were very old and worn. I could practically feel the scepticism baking off him. I stood awkwardly and wondered when I could make my exit. As if he had read my mind, the officer looked up at me and tilted his head towards the door. I opened my mouth to say something to Lucy, and then closed it and started to leave. If there was someone in the world who knew what to say in such a situation, they were not present in that room.

Mr Thompson seemed to age twenty years when I told him what had happened.

"Did the police say anything to you? Ask you anything?" he asked in his high-pitched voice. His face was pale and his eyes wide. Julie was there as well. God knows why she was there. Maybe they were an item on the down-low. Even if that was the case, right then both of them only had eyes for yours truly.

I shook my head. "Why?" I asked. Mr Thompson stared at me for a moment, and then grimaced.

"It's a murder house."

"What?" I blurted. Julie smiled, but it was a tight, mirthless smile. I was getting the idea she didn't like me much, if she had to start with. I guess I had gotten her in trouble. Some people just love a grudge, I suppose.

Thompson just shrugged. "It was a long time ago." He gave a funny little wave of his hand. "In that room, you know?" He stopped talking and just looked at me for a little bit. I just stared.

I mean, what was I going to say? What was I going to ask? I couldn't think of anything worse than standing there getting the sordid details from this pair of Stepford maniacs.

So I didn't ask anything, and I got the sense they were a little disappointed in my underdeveloped gossip muscle. In the end, Thompson just shrugged and pointed at the door. He was starting to look perky again. "Don't volunteer anything," he said to the back of my head as I left.

The plump police officer was standing at reception the next morning when I walked in.

"Morning," he said, and held out a hand. I shook it and tried not to look at his little moustache. It was wet. He had been sucking on it again.

"What's up?" I said, and then winced. "What can I do for you?" I amended. Smooth.

He sighed and then sucked on his moustache briefly. "Can you come and open that door again?" he asked.

"Why don't I just give you the key?" I replied, but he shook his head.

"No, no need really," he stopped, hesitated, and then spoke again. "She's gone missing. The mother, I mean."

So we went back. I didn't bother telling Thompson. The half-unpacked boxes were still on the kitchen floor, and the plates were still on the bench, but the place already felt empty. Unlived in. The corridor felt longer. It felt like I was sinking into that blue shag carpet as I followed the officer down the hall.

"Her work called it in. They knew what had happened with the daughter, of course. Her boss had tried to get hold of her to see how she was." He stopped at the door and gestured. I fished out the key and unlocked the door. We both pushed, and the door grudgingly moved inwards, accompanied by that unpleasant sound of wood squealing against wood. It was the same empty room. The officer stepped in and looked around, so I did the same. There was nothing.

The officer grunted. "Just needed to check," he said, and turned back to the door. I lingered. I'm not sure why. Maybe it was because of what Thompson had said. I stepped over to the window and peered at it. It was incredibly dirty. I looked closer. I could just make out rusty nail heads along the wooden base of the window frame. It had been nailed shut a long time ago.

I turned to go and had a moment of complete disorientation. The room lurched, and I sucked in air, hard. The door was slowly closing. Very slowly. I stared at it. I knew how hard it had been to push open. I had felt it grind against the floor as I put my weight against it, but now as I stared it was very slowly closing, smoothly, inch by inch, silently. I shook my head. The door continued its slow creep closed. I stepped towards it and I could swear I saw it give a little lurch, moving a few more inches in one movement. Without thinking, I grabbed the door frame and gave a tug backwards. Nothing happened, but I swear I felt a moment of resistance. I jerked again, and felt the small grinding vibration of the door scraping against the floor. I gave it another jerk, widening the gap enough to slip through and stepped out into the hallway. I stood there, breathing shakily.

"Lock that, would you?" the police officer said loudly from down the hall, and I screamed.

So here I sit, blunt pencil in hand, and a pile of what I hope are legible scribblings in a cheap notebook on the table. There are plates on the kitchen bench and half unpacked boxes on the floor. I have turned one light on so I can see what I've been writing, but I wish I didn't have to. The hallway is a black rectangle that I try not to look at. I strain, but can hear nothing.

How did I get from a screaming mess in the hallway to sitting here like this? I wish I could answer that properly.

It took a week for absolutely nothing to happen. Lucy did not reappear. Nor did her daughter. I eventually caved and asked Thompson for more information on the house, but he just shook his head and reminded me I needed to rent another property soon. I was back on borrowed time. I sat in my cramped little apartment that night and wondered why I was bothering. With the job. With anything, really.

Julie was more forthcoming. I guess she liked a gossip more

than she disliked me, but it was a pretty threadbare story. And Thompson had it wrong. There had been no real murder, it had just been assumed. I couldn't stop thinking about it. That house. That room. Betty, and Lucy, and that door slowly inching its way shut.

The house had been unoccupied for five years. It was the same owner now as then, a disinterested investor who used the place as a tax break. But it had to be a genuine rental for that, I guess, and someone had taken it up previously.

It had taken several days that last time before someone reported a missing person. The renter had been a young man, away from home for the first time—new job, new town, you know the deal. I tried to ignore the similarities, even as I looked at that toothy smile on Julie's face.

They searched the place. Thompson was the one who let them into the locked room. And there was nothing in there. Well, almost nothing, and that "almost" is where the murder rumour came from, I guess. When Thompson and a police officer pushed that door open, something fell to the floor. Thompson had bent down, but the officer had barked at him to stop. Stop and step back.

It was a fingertip. It was mashed up pretty badly from being wedged between the door and the doorframe. Crushed, like someone had not pulled their hand away quick enough when the door closed. Or had grabbed at the door as it closed, maybe. It turned out to belong to the young man who had rented the place, and a flurry of activity ensued. But there was no blood, no other trace evidence, nothing at all in that room except some dust and a dirty window. Eventually, things had died down.

That was then, and this is now. I guess things are settling down again, and quickly, but it doesn't seem like that in my head. I'm going to lose my job, I know that. I suck at it, and I don't have any drive to try and do it, anyhow. I guess I really don't care. I keep thinking of that door. How hard it was to push open, and how I caught it as it slowly swung shut. I think of my crappy apartment, and of Lucy's frantic expression when I last saw her. I think of my girlfriend, and

of that look of relief on her face when she kicked me to the curb. And I think of my parents, and how they had that same look on their face when I announced my exit from my childhood home. I wonder if Thompson and Julie will look like that if I don't come in to work.

I can't stop thinking about that room. I wonder if it is still empty when the door closes, and you are on the inside.

I lift my pencil from the page for a moment. I heard it just now, I'm sure. The click of a lock. It seems very loud in the dark house. I look towards the hallway. It is dark out there. Very dark, but in a moment, I will put the house keys on the table, and take myself down the hallway, and check that the door is now open. I'm sure it will be. And then I will go in. And then I will see.

The Cogwork Mermaid

Layla wiped away the last of her tears and looked down at the water. It churned and frothed around the pilings, the surface a deep grey laced in dirty white. Behind her, in another world, people laughed and shouted while children darted between the amusements of the cogwork park, screaming in delight.

In that world, a giant, shining dirigible hovered above the pier, casting a long shadow over those below. In that world, cogworks grinned and waved, hawking their wares and distractions and false promises. Well, she supposed they were cogworks, with their inflection-perfect chants ringing out over the heads of the milling, eager crowd. *Roll up, come see, everyone's a winner.* Perhaps some were actually real-life carnival folk, their pitches and actions passed from generation to generation until they glistened like fish hooks cast out amongst unwary fish.

Layla did not turn around. She had come for the dirigible launch, but she had turned away at the sight of its looming bulk. The old-timey rides and card sharps and clowns with bodies full of cogs that were the pier mainstays didn't interest her, either. Maybe they should have. Maybe it was her, not them. She was a murderer now, after all.

There was a bright flash, and Layla caught a glimpse of a bronze tail flicking the dirty grey water into clean white froth. The nearby steps led away from the crowd, away from the floating mass in the sky. She made her way down to the landing below the pier.

Some of the mermaids would talk to you for a coin or two, those that were equipped. Some even pretended to grant wishes, a thing from old stories that little kids adored and even some grown children might still seek. Other mermaids simply surged about, occasionally jumping high above the water and laughing, their scales flashing orange and blue and copper and a dozen other colours. They were usually popular, but today the landing was empty. The launching of the giant dirigible was probably too much of a draw for those who were not occupied by rides or sideshows. She had not been to see the mermaids in what seemed a lifetime herself. Most of them looked new, amazingly lifelike yet too bright and so very *there* as they jumped and splashed and carried on.

"Hello there," a bright, bubbly voice said.

The speaker leant on her elbows at the side of the landing, her chin cupped in her hands. Her hair was a wavy, bluish green, cut short to hang in wet locks to her jawline. Her small breasts were covered by a thin gauzy wrap, her alabaster skin dripping wet. Her long tail slapped lazily at the water. She was perfect.

Layla dug a coin from her pocket and handed it to the cogwork. The mermaid regarded it blankly, and then casually swallowed it without apparent effort.

"You look so beautiful," Layla said.

"Thank you," the mermaid replied, and reached up to touch her hair lightly. Her tail flicked and swished in the water. "What would you like to talk about?"

Layla frowned. She had been too caught up in chasing her own flittering thoughts to consider an actual conversation. Maybe she should tell the mermaid about her dead father, about the accident, the dirigible. Maybe she should say something about the aloof and bitter woman who had taken the place of her mother. Maybe speaking of those things would help. Maybe. Maybe it would just hurt.

"What's it like, being a mermaid?"

The mermaid smiled and flicked her tail again, as if to underline its existence.

"Do you want to know what it's like being a mermaid, or what it's like being a cogwork mermaid?"

"Oh," Layla said, hearing the disappointment in her own voice. "You know you are a cogwork?"

The mermaid's smile flattened a little.

"Yes, today I do. A young boy told me earlier. He laughed when he told me, and his friends laughed as well. He said his daddy builds new mermaids like me, and other things. He told me what happens in my own head, in my own body, like he was reciting a lesson that he had taken great pains to get right. He told me that tomorrow I won't remember. That my memory will be reset when I rest. That's what he said."

"Reset? Why?"

The mermaid tilted her head. Her tail splashed against the surface of the water again.

"Do you know I remember swimming in the deep ocean? When I close my eyes I can see a city of mermaids, diving and exploring and living our lives far away from here. I remember my family, and my friends, and I remember coming here to see the humans, to see people like you, to talk and wonder and have fun."

"What?" Layla asked, confused, but the mermaid just nodded, saltwater dripping from her nose.

"I miss my home, when I am here. The thought of my family is an ache inside. But I also know I am on an adventure, and that I will return home when I am done, so the missing is sweet, in its way."

She sighed. "I remember my parents, and my little sister, and the tall spire we lived in down below. And I suppose that is the point."

"What is?" Layla asked.

"Would you rather talk to a mermaid, one that is real and has a head full of memories, or a cogwork, a machine that considers the possible responses without even knowing it and then spits out the most pleasant?"

"But those memories are not real. They are just your programming," Layla said, and then flushed. There was no need to be cruel, even if it didn't really matter.

The mermaid cocked her head to one side.

"So I have my life, but none of it is real. And maybe I will be happier tomorrow, when I forget, and the people who come to talk to me will be happier as well. Maybe you should come back tomorrow."

Of course it didn't matter, but Layla couldn't help wondering what would be worse—finding out a whole life was false, just a set of pretend memories, or having that knowledge wiped away, returning to something happier but somehow less. It could happen again and again, and the mermaid would be powerless to do anything about it. She wouldn't even know. She looked at the beautiful cogwork and felt tears prick her own eyes.

"How do you know it isn't real?" Layla asked, not believing it—of course not—but suddenly wanting the mermaid to believe it could be.

The mermaid tilted her head a little in the other direction.

"How do you know this is?" she asked.

"Of course it's real," Layla said. She pointed up to where the looming shadow was mostly blocked by the pier.

"That will be the next luxury dirigible to traverse the ocean. My father built it. He died building it. That is what *real* is." She looked down and was surprised to see her hands balled into fists.

The mermaid nodded, ignoring Layla's anger, which made her even angrier. Mermaids were supposed to provide a pleasant little diversion, not upset people, not talk nonsense about life and memory. She started to turn away.

"Tell me about him," the mermaid said. Layla paused. She could tell the mermaid, she realised. It would be like telling no one. She turned back.

"He was a cogwork engineer." There was a sudden, painful lump high up in her chest.

"He got sick. All the engineers get sick eventually. The assembly might all be done by cogworks in the factories, but the *creating* is still a human job. The engineers are supposed to be safe, supposed to be in clean areas, but everyone knows the factories are dirty. Poison."

"Why do they do it, then?"

A question she couldn't answer. But the hot, burning lump in her chest was expanding, forcing more words out.

"He was going to make it. He was going to finish, and use the bonus money to buy the best medical treatments, to get himself fixed. He was so close!" She paused, her breath hitching. That lump had turned hard, cutting off her words.

The mermaid nodded as if she were listening. As if she could actually understand. It didn't matter, Layla thought. Tomorrow the mermaid won't even remember. The words won't have been said. It won't be real tomorrow.

"He was close. And then I stepped off the curb on the way to school and got hit by a damn cog-hauler, of all things. I should've seen it, or it should've stopped, but the stupid old cogwork driving it had one broken eye lens, was half blind, and it ran straight into me."

She drew a breath and reached up to touch the little scar below her ear. Such a small marker of such a large change. She had been thrown several feet by the impact, and her landing in the middle of the road had probably done more damage than the hauler had. She did not remember any of this—her father telling her was her first solid memory after the accident, his face grey and sad and thin as he spoke, holding her hand as she lay in bed.

"He looked so much sicker when he told me about the accident," Layla said softly. "I had lost weeks, but he had lost more. Mother said he had not been able to work on the dirigible— had not been able to concentrate on anything else until I was better. He ran out of time because of me. I killed him."

She knew it was what her mother thought. She could see it simmering just below the surface of every word, every action, every tear-filled, hate-filled glance. This was the first time she had said it out loud herself—given voice to what she knew was true. And yet that hot lump in her chest had not lessened with the words.

"So you feel guilty?" the mermaid asked. She looked only mildly curious, and Layla felt another flash of anger.

"What would you know—" she began, but the mermaid cut her off with a splash of her tail and a sunny smile.

"You know, mermaids can grant wishes to those they deem worthy."

Layla stared at the cogwork. Back on the pier there was cheering and a loud, braying horn—three long, hollow calls heralding the dirigible's launch. That was what she had come to see, but now she barely registered it.

"Have you slipped a cog?"

The mermaid laughed, a tinkling of programmed amusement. "Humour me. Tonight I will be reset and tomorrow if I offer someone a wish, I will think I am real, and that my offer is real. So for now, let's play make-believe while we both know better. What would you wish for, if you had one wish?"

Layla felt her anger and irritation start to fade, leaving only that aching lump in her chest. It was all just programming and cogs, but in a way, the mermaid would die tonight. Not completely, but a part of her would be gone, and tomorrow she would be different. Different, like Layla was after the accident, after her father's death. After the way her mother looked at her.

She thought of the dirigible again, and of her tears when she had seen it floating there, shining and huge, the brass and steel and windows all flashing like diamonds, while its shadow fell over her. The last, largest impression her father would ever leave on the world. She showed the mermaid her own small, sad smile.

"Okay. I wish I was not responsible for my father's death. I wish he had not died because of me."

"Done!" the mermaid said without pause, and splashed her tail hard against the surface of the dirty grey water so shining droplets flew every which way. Layla laughed despite herself, half in shock, half in embarrassment, and scattered a few fresh tears with a shake of her head.

"And how do you propose to do that?"

The mermaid's smile faltered.

"Do you really, truly want that?"

Layla hesitated without really knowing why. It was ridiculous—it was just a cogwork, after all. It wasn't real. None of it. She nodded.

"You asked how I knew I was a cogwork? How I knew the boy who said so was telling the truth?"

Layla said nothing. There was a long moment in which the mermaid just looked at her, her smile gone, her face solemn. And then she reached up with one perfect alabaster hand and brushed aside a wet lock of her hair. There, bright against her pale skin, was a small, raised scar. Layla lifted a hand and touched the identical one under her own ear.

"It's a maintenance port," the cogwork mermaid said very quietly. She glanced back at a couple of other mermaids that were diving in and out of the water, laughing. "All the latest models have them."

Layla opened her mouth and then closed it slowly. Her mind was suddenly a blank—just like when she tried to recall her accident, or her hospital stay. All she could recall was her father's thin, sad smile as he sat by her bed, and later, the blame in her mother's face. Her father had not stopped working after the accident, she realised—he had just stopped working on the dirigible.

"But I have a whole life…" she began, and then stopped. The mermaid's smile had returned, but it was bitter, now. Very bitter. Layla reached up and touched her scar again.

"You did it," she said. "You granted my wish." The lump in her chest was gone. Behind her, in that other world, the horn sounded again and people cheered. Layla watched the shadow of the dirigible start to move across the water, to move away, and her mouth twisted in a smile to match the mermaid's.

The cogwork started to slide backward off the landing, slipping almost soundlessly into the water.

"Yes," the mermaid said. "For today."

Beach Memories

I blink in surprise. Sure, the summer sun is hot and bright and glints off the water, but I don't think it should make the whitewash look that pale pink colour. But then the next wave crashes and whatever it was disappears.

It's only a tiny stretch of beach, but it's still surprising there are not a few more people. There were several cars parked in the wide clearing just over the dunes, and I can see two piles of belongings on the little beach as well, towels and bags and an umbrella that has fallen sideways, but the owners are not in evidence. There is an old couple a little way from me, though. She is wearing a big floppy hat, and they lay out their beach gear with the unconscious synchronicity of lifelong partners. The old guy smiles at her in an absent sort of way. It's sweet, but for some reason it makes me uneasy, like I'm forgetting something important.

There is one other group that has just arrived. A family. Mum, dad, a teenage girl. As I'm watching the girl laughs and runs from mum, her long brown hair streaming out behind her. She dives into the water, straight into a cresting wave, and just for a moment I'm sure the foaming water flashes pink again. She doesn't come up.

Her mother falters in her pursuit, looks around for a moment, and then turns back to Dad. She says something and they both laugh and flop down onto their towels. I stare at them and then at the small, breaking waves. The girl doesn't surface.

Mum lays back and closes her eyes. Dad reaches into a bag

and pulls out a paperback. Just down from them the old woman, *sans* hat, is thigh deep in the water. I take a few steps towards Mum and Dad, looking between them and the water. The girl has been under for a long time.

"Hey!" I call.

Dad looks up from his book.

"Yes?" he asks. "Can I help you?"

I take a few more steps towards them, glancing pointedly at the water as I do so.

"You…ah…aren't worried? She's been under for a long time now."

Dad has the same brown hair and open, honest face as his grinning daughter, but he isn't smiling.

"Who?"

Now Mum is sitting up and looking at me curiously.

"Your daughter. She dove in."

Dad's frown deepens, but it's Mum who responds. "We don't have a daughter."

I don't know what to say. Then it makes sense and I shake my head. They are wasting time.

"Whoever the girl was. Is."

It's Dad that replies this time, and there is a guarded note to his voice as he slowly stands up.

"We are here alone."

I stare at them both and they stare back. Finally I look down and see something. I point.

"You have three towels laid out."

Mum looks down at the three towels. One with red stripes, one green, one blue. Obviously a set, but she shakes her head.

"I don't know who owns that red towel."

They look at each other and I can read their thoughts loud and clear. They think I'm a crazy person.

"Look," I say, pointing out at the water, "I don't know what is going on, but a girl dove in and hasn't come up. I thought she was with you. You chased her." Even as I say it I realise how weird it sounds. Dad looks at Mum and then he bends and grabs their towels. He leaves the third one, but I notice Mum's gaze seems to slide away from that red striped towel, like she doesn't want to see it.

I look past them. The old woman is now standing a little deeper in the water, but she is watching us. Her husband has done one better, and come on over.

"Ask them," I say.

Dad frowns at me and then turns. When I look again the old lady is gone, and I get a glimpse of pink foam as a wave breaks where she had been standing.

"Them?" the old man says as he steps up next to Dad. "I'm here by myself."

I argue, of course. I point out the big bag and the floppy straw hat sitting with the old guy's gear down the beach.

"Not mine," he says, but I can see him frown a little. Just like the mum, his gaze slides away from the unclaimed beach accoutrements and back to me.

"You are scaring these nice people," he says.

Mum and Dad nod, but I'm not paying them much attention. I'm looking at the water, the small, crashing waves and the foaming white wash. There are no flashes of pink. There is still no girl, and no old lady. And I am scared, too.

My hands shake as I unlock my car. I keep seeing the way Mum didn't want to see that red striped towel, and the way the old man's eyes slid away from that floppy straw hat. I keep seeing those flashes of pink.

As I settle into the driver's seat I realise I've left whatever I took to the beach back down there on the sand. I'm thinking about going back when my gaze settles on something else. It takes a moment for me to register what I'm looking at - a lipstick case sitting in the console between the front seats. That feeling of forgetting something has come back, and as I stare at the lipstick all I can think of is that first pink flash of foam on the water. I glance in the rear vision mirror, but then I let my gaze slide away. I know I came to the beach alone. I know I'm single. And there is no reason I know for a child's booster seat to be in the back of my car.

Guess Who's Coming To Christmas Dinner?

"**H**e's bringing a girl!"

My mother is standing at the kitchen bench, a light dusting of flour down her apron, the tray of warm cookies almost forgotten in her hands. She is so happy. Christmas is her thing. The house smells like nutmeg and cinnamon and pine needles. There is tinsel and holly and every year a tree so large it looks like the house was built around it. She has been in a whirlwind of preparation, cooking and wrapping gifts and almost bursting with her news.

Dad is still knocking the snow from his shoes in the entrance. He grunts.

"I said, he's bringing a *girl*!"

"I heard you," he replies, and ruffles my hair as he comes into the kitchen. He kisses my mother on her red cheek and snags a cookie, ignoring her squawk of protest. He grins at me and sits at the table.

"I think it will snow more tonight, kiddo," he says. I'm staring out the window at all the white. I can see the Sheldon kids coming out of their house across the street with their sleds. They'll be heading for Pike's Hill, which is the best sled run on this side of town. For a moment I think about hurrying to join them, but I want to see Pete. He's been at college for just about forever, and listening to him on the phone is not the same. I miss my big brother.

Mum slides a hot cup of coffee in front of him and Dad leans back and sighs. He's off work now. Despite all of Mum's crazy preparations, it never really feels like Christmas until Dad is on break. He feels it too—he says he can't get into holiday mode until the office is closed.

"So, kiddo, what did you ask Santa for?"

"Can you not call her *kiddo?*" Mum says a little peevishly. "She's almost a teenager."

"Oh, God forbid!" Dad says, and rolls his eyes.

"I don't mind," I say. "But Dad, you know I don't believe in Santa anymore. That's little kids' stuff."

"Ah, I see."

"I said he's bringing a girl! Charles, did you hear me?"

Dad laughs. I like it a lot when he laughs. His wrinkles turn to crinkles and he looks a lot younger. After a moment Mum laughs too. She knows he has been letting her stew. He's good at winding her up.

"A girl. Our Pete has a girl. Fancy that."

"It must be serious," Mum says. She is excited, but a little wary. I am, too.

"How serious can it be, if we've never even heard of her?" Dad asks, and sips his coffee. He doesn't seem that phased.

"But she's coming for Christmas!" Mum replies.

Dad grins again. "Oh no, you might run out of cookies!"

Mum has put Dad to work stirring something in the kitchen, so when the car pulls up I am the first to the door. I reef it open just as Pete is reaching for the doorknob.

"Hey, it's the little jerk!" he laughs, and steps forward to sweep me up into a hug.

"Oof," he says, and puts me down. "You are getting too heavy for that!"

"Never!" I laugh. Pete looks good. Happy. He is maybe a bit thinner than when he left all those months ago, and he has a new haircut which is either ridiculous or cool, I can't tell which, but otherwise he is the same old Pete. I feel a bit of relief, which is kind of surprising. I didn't realise I was worried that he would be different.

He steps aside.

"Scarlett, meet the little jerk. Jerk, meet Scarlett."

For a moment I don't know what to say. She is beautiful, but nothing like I imagined—nothing like Pete's few high school girlfriends. She is small, shorter even than Mum, but very thin. She is so pale her skin almost matches the snow, but her hair is a deep, deep red, and her lips are as well. She smiles, and her teeth are perfect. That is not something I've ever noticed on someone before. Perfect teeth. I realise I am staring.

"Hi," I say, and stick out my hand. "I'm Catherine. Cat."

Scarlett steps forward and grips my hand firmly.

"Hello," she says, and her voice is silky smooth. "It's lovely to meet you. I must confess to feeling a bit nervous. Christmas is usually a solitary time for me."

I smile. "Don't be nervous. You've met the worst of us already if you know Pete."

She laughs, and it's like chiming silver bells. She's delightful.

My parents think she is delightful as well. And Pete—well, it's pretty clear what Pete thinks. He keeps touching her, which is cute, but kind of, well, gross as well. Bedroom stuff, maybe.

Mum serves up a heaping plate of her cinnamon Christmas cookies and everyone sits at the kitchen table. Pete is telling everyone how he and Scarlett met. I should be paying attention, and I am trying, but for some reason it's hard. Mum and Dad are smiling and nodding, and Pete is laughing, and Scarlett is too, but it feels a little strange. Mum and Dad and Pete all look a little puzzled, like they are having trouble focusing on their own conversation. I take a sip of my milk (no coffee for *youngsters*, like every second thing in the world isn't jammed full of caffeine anyway) and almost gag. I spit the milk back into the glass.

"Cat!" Mum almost snaps.

"Sorry Mum, but the milk is gross!"

"What?" Mum grabs my glass and sniffs, and then wrinkles up her nose. "Oh, dear." She reaches for Dad's coffee. "Don't drink that, dear, the milk has gone bad."

Dad looks down at his coffee, and I glance as well. Even from where I'm sitting I can see large yellowish lumps floating on the surface.

"Funny," Dad says. "It seemed okay earlier."

Pete laughs and hands his cup to Mum. "Lucky you are dairy intolerant, Scarlett!"

She laughs and smiles and I can see Mum relax. But it's odd, too. I had thought Scarlett's teeth were perfect. Now, as she laughs, they look a bit crooked. And a bit yellow. But she is still a delight.

Mum's low-key Christmas craziness presents itself in many ways. One is the strict routine of Christmas Eve, masquerading as a casual wind-down to a lazy Christmas day. We all know what is expected. While Pete and Scarlett canoodle on the couch, watching as Dad tries to light the fire, I put yet more of Mum's cinnamon cookies on a plate. When the doorbell rings we all converge in the entrance. Scarlett looks curious.

"What's this?" she asks me. I'm about to answer when Mum opens the door and the carollers start up with "O Come, All Ye Faithful". There are only four of them, rugged up with scarves and beanies and jackets, and there is a light dusting of fresh snow on their shoulders. The youngest one, a pink-faced boy my own age that I kind of know from school, is grinning with embarrassment but singing anyway.

Two things happen then—one is as expected as the cinnamon in the cinnamon cookies the carollers are about to get. The other is more shocking than the fact that the cookies are sugar-free. Mum claps her hands and exclaims in delight, because "Faithful" is one of her favourites (although the list is long and not that exclusive). At the same time, Scarlett hisses and draws back from the open door. I glance at her curiously, but I'm the only one that does. Pete and my parents don't seem to notice.

"I don't like carols," she says, looking at me with a curl to her lip that makes her look…well, not quite like a delight. Her teeth are definitely yellow, and it must just be the afternoon light, but her skin is a bit sallow as well. She moves back to the lounge room quietly. Silently, even, and no one watches her go but me.

"I have my own stocking," Scarlett says to Mum. "Would you mind if I hang it with yours?"

Mum smiles, and I'm pretty sure Scarlett's stock just went up significantly. Anyone who brings their own stocking for Christmas must have at least a sprinkle of my mother's craziness for the holiday.

"Of course, dear, how lovely. Go ahead."

We are all sitting in the lounge room. It's dark outside, and Mum has the lights turned down so we can appreciate Dad's smouldering fire and the flickering lights that are trying valiantly to span the girth of the tree. Scarlett approaches the mantel and moves the large snow globe with the very inaccurate depiction of a snowy nativity to one side. She pouts a little as she rearranges our stockings slightly, and then all of a sudden there is a huge burlap sack hanging there in front of the fire. It is brown and old and dirty, and I have no idea where it came from. It just kind of…appeared.

I stare, but Pete and my parents just nod and smile.

"How lovely," my mother says.

Scarlett smiles and then looks at me. My question about her "stocking" dies in my throat. Her skin is definitely off-white, a greyish yellow, and I swear her nose is a bit more crooked than I had thought. Her smile fades and she gives me an odd, speculative look before heading back to the couch and snuggling up with my brother. It all suddenly feels a bit less than delightful.

I wake in the night. I don't know why. I've never been one for being overexcited on Christmas Eve, but there is definitely… something. A heavy, expectant feeling in the air. I slip out of bed and head downstairs, carefully avoiding the riser three from the bottom, the one that creaks like a tired old tabby cat getting stepped on.

It doesn't matter. Scarlett is sitting on the couch, watching the doorway as I appear. The only light comes from the flickering, dying flames around Dad's giant log that he swore was not too large.

"Hello," she says quietly. Her voice is not as pleasant as it was.

It sounds a bit like the creaky stair. Her hair is still red, even in the feeble orange light, but it is hanging in thin strands with lots of pale scalp showing. She smiles at me, and her teeth are long and crooked and kind of sharp.

"What are you?" I say. It's not what I meant to ask. Actually, I had no idea what I'd meant to ask. My brain seems to have stopped working.

"Ah. I thought you might be able to see me. It's the look of surprise, you know, that gives people away." She nods, looking thoughtful as she raises one very long finger and scratches at her bent nose. "My power always wanes a little around now. Too long without feeding."

I want to turn around and go back to my room. The only thing stopping me is the thought of what this thing might do if I try to leave.

Scarlett sighs. "Sit."

I move forward on wooden legs. I don't want to, but I can't seem to help myself. I sit down opposite Scarlett, in Dad's chair. No one else is allowed to sit in it, but honestly, I'm not that worried about one of his grumpy looks right now.

"I'm not going to hurt you, Cat. My kind don't eat children." She makes a face. "Well, some do, but not me. I'm a special case."

"What are you?" I ask again.

Scarlett scratches her nose again, and then smiles. Her teeth look very large and sharp in the dim firelight and I'm pretty sure her gums are bleeding.

"I'm a Christmas Witch."

A silence falls, and she looks at me expectantly. No, not expectantly. Hopefully. After a long, drawn out moment she sighs again.

"Oh, dear. I was famous, you know, once upon a time. All through the Mountains of Vlachs, and even in parts of the Byzantine Empire."

"What do you want?"

Scarlett smiles again, and I shudder. She seems about to say something when there is a thumping on the roof. She raises one hand and makes a funny little gesture, and I can't speak. Can't even open my mouth.

Very quietly, Scarlett gets up and creeps towards the dying fire. Even as she moves, there is another thump from above, and then a shower of soot falls down onto Dad's weak fire. There is a flash of red in the fireplace, and then Scarlett moves so quickly I can barely follow her. She grabs her huge sack from the mantel and pounces. There is a muffled yell, and then she is tying the top of the bag tight with a piece of rope. The bag heaves this way and that, and then another yell bursts forth. Scarlett starts kicking the bag viciously with one long, thin foot.

"Shut up!" she hisses. She kicks again, and there is a low groan from inside the bag.

She looks at me and grins a hideous, bloody grin, and I can suddenly talk again. I draw breath to scream.

"I wouldn't," she says very quietly.

She kicks the bag again, almost absently, and then makes a funny gesture at me. I yawn, and then blink a few times and look around. I'm in the lounge room with my brother's girlfriend.

"I think you've been sleepwalking, dear," Scarlett says sweetly. "Off to bed with you."

The presents are done, the adults have had their coffee (black— the new milk has also gone bad for some reason), and we are about to sit down to Christmas dinner. Mum is the happiest I've ever seen her, and that is saying something. She is usually almost paralysed with good will and cheer on Christmas, but this is a whole other level. It might have something to do with Scarlett insisting she help cook.

We sit down. The table is almost groaning under the weight of the food. There is gravy and greens and potatoes and cranberry sauce. There are Dad's favourite pickles, the ones that are made from vegetables that have no right ever being pickled, like cauliflowers and carrots, and in the middle of the table, a long rolled roast. For just a moment I wonder what it is. But that doesn't matter—it smells so wonderful, like meat, but also kind of like pudding and cookies and spices and eggnog and, well, all of Christmas. Scarlett smiles as she hands the carving knife to Dad, and I feel my mouth watering as I watch the knife slip into the pink, almost bloody flesh.

We all fall silent for a while, and the only sound to be heard is chewing. Finally, Mum pauses.

"That's just marvellous. It has a flavour I can't quite put my finger on."

Scarlett swallows and nods. "It's an old family recipe. A special Christmas treat."

My mother smiles a little shyly. "And do you think Santa might bring me the recipe?"

Scarlett laughs, tossing her head back, her perfect white teeth gleaming.

"I don't think Santa will be dropping by this house next year," I say, and swallow. My parents and Pete look at me curiously, and I blush. I don't know why I said that.

Scarlett laughs again, and for a moment it looks like her mouth is full of blood.

"Oh, he will. I'm sure of it. I mean, there must be a lot of Santas to visit everyone in one night. Surely one will pop in."

She speared another piece of meat on her plate.

"Maybe you and I could stay up and wait for him, Cat."

I smile. She really is delightful.

On The Big Screen

Mum is in her workshop when the lights start flickering. I am hanging out by the door. Sometimes she tells me to go away, with her cranky face on. But mostly she doesn't mind.

"Hey kiddo," she says as she comes out and touches my hair. I like it when she does that, it feels like everything is normal again. "Think it's Dad again? Or just the batteries?"

Mum sometimes goes in and pokes at the big batteries in the garage and swears, but I think this time it's Dad. I don't say so, though. I hate it when they fight, and they fight more and more now. Mum says it's because they are stressed from the lockdown, and from being stuck inside—especially Dad. She says not to worry about it, and that of course they still love each other. Dad says it's all because Mum won't listen to him.

I know a lot about the lockdown. Dad constantly runs the televisions in the house, and all he watches is the news. Mum says it is not helping him to get over things, to brood like that. I don't know what she means. We had chickens that used to get broody, but they are all dead now. They were all floppy and bleeding yesterday, and Mum yelled at me to stop touching them. That was scary.

The TV is pretty scary now, too. It's just things on fire, people yelling, tanks and big ships. I miss *Bluey*, even though it's just for little kids, and I miss *Horrible Histories*. But those channels are just black-and-white fuzz now, even when Dad says I can try them.

Mum goes down the hall. I'm not supposed to go in unless

they say it's okay, but I can hear from the hallway pretty good. "You have to let me go, Audrey." That's Dad. His voice sounds flat and kind of sad, but it always does a bit since he went away.

"Just give me a little more time," Mum says. It's what she always says.

"You know it won't work. You are probably the smartest person left alive, but it took you nearly ten years to build that first motherboard, not to mention the server and the rest. And that was when you could order parts."

"I'll finish it," Mum says.

"And then what?" Dad says. It sounds like he is crying.

She doesn't say anything. After a bit she comes out and touches my hair.

"It was nothing, honey. Go in and say hi."

Dad is on the big screen. His face is all stretched out with super-big lips and eyes that don't blink. I hate the big screen. Sometimes I dream about it, only it's my face on there, all stretched out like that.

"Hey kiddo," he says, and smiles. I try to smile back but it's hard.

"Your Mum's not real happy with me," he says, but he keeps smiling. Sometimes I don't understand that, when grown- up faces don't match the words. It's not just the screen; Mum does it too.

"Why do you keep doing things like that to the lights?" I ask.

He sighs. "Oh, buddy, it's hard to explain." He sighs again, and then looks away. The screen flickers. Sometimes it does that, when Dad gets sad, or angry. "I didn't ask for this."

I've heard him say that before. Sometimes I've heard him yell it at Mum, and then she yells back. Sometimes she cries. Sometimes she comes out of the room with her cranky face on.

Thinking of all that makes me sad, and I feel a bit funny in my tummy. I look away from Dad and sniff. I don't want him to see me cry.

"Hey," he says, his voice soft. "Don't worry about it. It's just Mum and Dad stuff."

I try to wipe away the tears. It feels like a lot of wetness, and when I drop my hand it is smeared with red. There is a lot of it. I feel funnier, and when I look up at Dad, he looks all red too.

"Christ!" Dad swears. He never swears. His face flickers and disappears, and then reappears.

"Audrey!" he screams. Every speaker in the house screams.

I sit down. I can hear running feet.

"Oh God! Oh God!" I can hear Mum saying, and then I'm lifted up.

"Audrey, you'll catch it!" Dad shouts, and Mum laughs, but it doesn't sound like a happy laugh.

"Does it matter?" she says, her voice all wobbly, and she hugs me too tight. It hurts. I feel like I'm going to be sick, but when I open my mouth just red stuff comes out. It gets all over Mum. She is crying. Dad is yelling something. Mum is shaking her head. I throw up again. It really hurts.

"You know what you have to do, Audrey," Dad says from the big screen.

"I can't," Mum cries, hugging me. "You were right. There's no parts for another board."

"Not that," Dad says. "Please, please don't do that. Let him go. Let us go."

"I can't," Mum says again. "I won't."

There is no sound for a bit. My throat hurts, and the front of my shirt feels sticky. I feel very sleepy. You are supposed to sleep when you are sick—it helps you get better.

Mum is running one hand through my hair. It feels nice. I like it when she does that.

"Audrey," Dad says, but his voice is far away. "Let him go."

When I wake up my throat doesn't hurt. Nothing hurts; I'm all better. I try to look around for Mum, but I can't seem to move.

I'm in the lounge room—Dad's room. But it's all wrong.

I can see the TV, down low on the far wall, and I can see the door. But I can't see the big screen.

Mum comes in and smiles at me. She has to lift her head up to do it, which is strange. She comes close and reaches out to touch my hair, but I can't feel anything. I feel a bit panicky.

"Mum," I say, and my voice is super loud. "Where's Dad?"

She smiles at me, but I think it's one of those grown-up smiles that aren't about being happy.

"I only had one board," she says.

"I don't understand," I say, but I think I do. It is like when Dad got sick and Mum took him into the workshop. I start to cry, and somewhere down the hall some lights start flickering.

Jericho And The Cursed Forest

It was obvious the forest was cursed. The trees were squat and thick and crowded together, and sometimes when you weren't looking right at them they would get up and move around, as if they could feel eyes upon them and found it disagreeable. The leaves of these trees were strange and irregular and mismatched, but all were dark and oily and liked to shiver when the air was still. Unlike the wide road on the other side of the village, there was only a thin path that continued on past the houses and into the trees, and no one was sure where it might lead. Certainly none of the many adventurers who came to the village looking to break the curse knew where the path went—or if it went anywhere.

The forest made Jericho more uneasy than it did the rest of the villagers. Sometimes, when he was cutting the wood that came in wagons down the wide road instead of the forest that was right there, he would feel the nearby trees shivering their leaves at him. They would *lean*, deep and dark and pressing in on his awareness, the sound of the leaves filling his ears. Sometimes the whispering would be full of words, full of meaning just for him, but when he listened closer there would be nothing, and then his whole world would be empty, just the chopping of wood and the dusty streets and the sinking sun, and the forest would just *be*, so large, so unknown, and there. Right there.

When that happened Jericho would put his axe down and go amongst the older villagers and ask about the forest—of the curse, of the trees, of the many adventurers who'd passed that way, never to return. And some of the villagers would look at him with pity, and some with understanding, and some with impatience, but none would answer him.

Jericho's mother was the village baker, and she was known for the evenness of her loaves and the fairness of her prices. She was also known for her patience with Jericho, who was sometimes like a pebble from the road that has gotten into a shoe, if the pebble would not stop asking questions.

"Ma," he asked one day, after the forest had been whispering at him, "what is the curse, really? I mean, it's obvious there is a curse, but what is it? No one will say."

He was sitting by the door, watching a young man with yellow hair discuss something important with the smith. He knew what was being said was important, because the man pushed his chest out and gestured with his smooth, pale hands. A lot of the young men and women that came looking for the curse talked and gestured like that. Sometimes they wore fine cloaks with tasselled edges and had a horse, like the man he was watching now. Sometimes they wore shirts of homespun brown and walked in worn shoes, and did not have a horse to lodge with the smith. But always they asked the villagers about the curse, or the forest, or if any of those that had come before had returned from the too-narrow path that disappeared between the misshapen trees.

They asked the same questions Jericho asked, and they received no answers.

His mother was kneading dough. She kneaded dough often, which was fine with Jericho. She could not easily escape his questions when she was kneading.

"Why is it obvious the forest is cursed?" his mother asked. She often answered Jericho's questions with another question.

"Well, it is, isn't it?" he said. "Everyone always says so, and it looks…" He stopped, knowing she knew everything he did.

"None of the adventurers ever come back," he said instead.

"One of them might," she said. "You never know."

"Would the forest be safe if someone broke the curse?"

"Would the wider world be better off if that happened?" his mother asked.

He thought this was also something they both knew.

"That man with the yellow hair said he must break the curse," Jericho said next. "I heard him. *Must*, he said. Not *might*."

At this his mother stopped kneading. She turned her dark eyes on him, and there was a smear of white flour on her cheek. There was love in her look, and patience, and a shadow that may have been thoughts of the forest, or the curse, or her boy's questions.

"Most people don't understand how empty words can be. It is a hard thing to learn, how to listen to words. To decide if the words that are used are empty or full."

His mother had said that before. Jericho didn't really understand. The only thing he was sure of was that he had watched the adventurers come to the village and go down the path between the trees of the forest, and he had asked all the people of the village about the forest, and the trees, and the path. But the villagers did not talk about the forest, or the curse, and he never got any answers that were really proper answers. His mother was not helping.

He made his decision, which he had thought perhaps he had made a long time ago but never let himself realise.

"I want to try."

His mother's face went as white as the flour smeared on her cheek, but she said nothing. It was perhaps too large a thing he had asked, but it was also something she may have been expecting. The village was next to the forest, after all. She had seen him standing and watching the leaves, his head cocked, the wood axe dangling limply in one hand. She knew the questions he asked.

She went back to kneading, and when eventually she did speak, her voice was mostly steady.

"Get me another bag of flour, would you?"

Later that day an adventurer came to the bakery, which was really only the front half of the front room of their little house. The girl was not much older than Jericho, and was small and quiet and had brown hair that had been cut short very unevenly. She asked for three loaves of the small, hard travel bread that might hurt your teeth but would keep in the bottom of a leather bag until you forgot you even had them. Jericho put them on the wooden board they used as a benchtop, but when he told her the price she pushed one back towards him. He was not surprised. Adventurers only came in two types, and this girl did not have a horse or a tasselled cloak.

"Why do you think you can break the curse?" he asked. He thought he knew what she would say—that to break the curse would be a good thing. A good thing for the forest. For the world.

"Just because," she said.

He still did not understand what his mother meant about the fullness and emptiness of words, but he didn't need to understand, to know the girl had told him nothing.

He pushed the third loaf across the bench and waved her coins away.

"I'll bring more food," he said, "if I can come too."

In the morning Jericho woke as always, with the stars still spilling across the dark sky and dawn less of a reality than the glowing orange of the banked ovens. He tended the first bake with his mother, and if she noticed the extra wood he had cut and put aside, she did not speak of it, and if she thought he was unusually quiet, she did not comment. But when he told her he was poorly and might need to take himself to his bed to rest, she went to the pile of old burlap sacks and pulled out his rolled blanket and the bag he had filled with bread and cheese.

"I put some apples in there," she said. "And don't forget your waterskin."

Jericho took the blanket and the bag, and his mother began crying. He hugged her, and she held him very tightly for a time.

"Listen," she said, wiping her eyes with one hand. "You must listen."

Jericho nodded, but she did not say anything else. She just looked at him, and then gave him a gentle push towards the door.

The path into the forest was so narrow and twisting that the smith made much from the stabling of adventurers' horses, and more from the eventual claiming of each, but it was just wide enough for Jericho and the girl to walk side by side if they did not mind the closeness.

The girl did not speak as they crossed into the shadow of the trees, and she did not look up when the leaves overhead shivered.

"They do that," Jericho finally said, just to be saying something. It made him feel helpful, even though he did not really know what it was the trees did.

They walked for a time in silence, and both were grateful of the other's nearness. The trees shifted behind them, and to the sides, and the dark leaves shivered and shivered.

The girl looked back over her shoulder.

"The trees have taken the path away," she said. Her voice trembled a little.

Jericho did not look back. There did not seem to be any point.

"What is your name?" he asked instead.

"Thither," the girl said. They trod the pale path for a dozen more heartbeats before she spoke again.

"Hither and Thither and Yon," she said. "And I am the middle of the three. Goatherds in a village with barely more goats than minders. Hither does not need my help, and Yon is content enough to sing and natter to the piebald she-goat so she doesn't stray."

She spoke as if she could talk the trees still. She spoke as if she were trying to answer the question Jericho had asked before, in the bakery.

"I heard of the forest, and I decided to come. It was something I decided for myself. It was for myself," she said. "By myself," she added. Her voice caught, as if she wanted to say more but dare not, and she looked at Jericho as if she had just realised he was there.

Jericho wasn't sure what that meant, but he listened, and he thought her words did not sound empty. Not this time.

They came to a place where a tree had fallen. It had left a large hole to one side of the path, rich black earth torn up in hunks like strange fists reaching for the sky. The trunk blocked the path, long and thick and dark, with fat mushrooms growing from the bark in bluish clumps that looked both strong and strange. Where the fallen crown of branches lay, spread all out in a stillness of leaves, other trees stood and bent down low. Their leaves were a susurrus of melancholy.

Jericho opened his bag and took out two round loaves studded with walnuts and dried apricots. He had cut the apricots himself, and they made the bread both sweet and a little bitter.

They ate their bread in silence. They had been walking all morning, and Jericho wanted to sit on the fallen tree, but he stood on the path instead. As they finished eating, the shivering of the leaves of the crowded trees grew into a rustling.

"Someone is coming," Thither said. She was looking at the trees that had been crowded around the fallen one. They had stilled suddenly, trunks and leaves.

Jericho had not heard anything, but when he looked to the still trees he saw a bird. It was small, and twitched and darted like the brown robins that gathered for the stale seeds behind the bakery.

This robin was black, with a bright red beak. It was very thin, and poorly, with some missing feathers. It hopped from the tree it was in to the branches of the fallen tree.

"It's only a bird," Jericho said, trying to pretend it was not the first black robin with a red beak he had ever seen, nor the first bird he had seen in the forest trees, even those at the very edge of the village.

Another bird joined the first, and then a third. Then suddenly there were more, many more, lining the branches of the downed tree like they were standing guard, or mourning, or seeking more than empty words to fill their small stomachs. Some were missing feathers, and others had dull beaks and cloudy eyes. They were silent, but the leaves of some of the trees shivered once more, and a few of the squat trunks shifted enough that

Jericho could see between them.

Thither was right. Someone was coming. They had yellow hair, and a cloak with tassels.

"Hello?" Thither called. The fancy adventurer who had talked of important things with the village smith did not reply. He came on, slowly but steadily. His eyes were clear and sharp, and he held his hands out in front of him, palms upwards.

"He is bleeding," Thither whispered.

She was right. His cupped hands brimmed with his own blood. Jericho drew back, and the adventurer smiled.

"I am feeding the birds," he said.

There was something in his face that Jericho did not understand. It was both like and not like the look he had had in the village, when he gestured to the smith and talked so urgently. It was almost like the look he had had when he said he must break the curse.

Must.

"Do…do you feed them because you must?" Jericho asked.

The black robins flew up in twos and threes, alighting on the edges of the pale hands and dipping their beaks into the small pool of blood. When each had drunk their fill they flew away, and more fluttered up to line the sides of the adventurer's palms. Some were so weak they could not fly, and these climbed his legs, pulling themselves up with their beaks and claws.

The trees shifted, and the leaves dipped down to shiver above all of their heads.

"No," the yellow-haired man said. "No, but I think it is important."

"You are hurt," Thither said, but softly.

The birds dipped their beaks into the man's blood, and drank, and flew. Others came.

"Things I did before. Things I said," the man said with a very small smile. "I thought they were important, but they never hurt. This might be better."

The yellow-haired man refused any offers to bandage his hands, or to take him further along the path away from the birds.

He did not need to go anywhere, he said. He was helping the birds. Feeding them.

So Jericho and Thither walked on, away from the fallen tree and the red-beaked birds and the man with his cupped palms of blood and his small hurt he was offering up for the first time.

"We should have helped him," Thither said after some time, when the path had twisted and turned and the trees had shifted as if the forest and the way through danced with each other.

"I don't think he needed it," Jericho said. He was listening to the leaves all around, and thinking of how some words sounded empty, and some did not. The man's words had not sounded empty. The shivering of the leaves overhead did not, although he still could not understand them.

Thither looked at him, and then nodded.

"For himself," she said, as if that made sense. "By himself."

They walked on, and when they were thirsty, and hungry, they drank from their waterskins and ate bread and cheese from Jericho's bag but they did not stop.

Eventually the path started down a low slope, and now the trees drew away and the path turned back on itself as it went, snaking around rocky outcrops and older fallen trees where the undergrowth clustered in fever-thick growths.

At the bottom of the slope there was a stream that was almost a river. The path led straight into it, and started again on the other side. The water ran fast and deep across the path, with dangerous eddies and spinning currents.

They stopped.

"Look," Thither said, and pointed.

Upstream there was a tiny boat moored to a pointed rock on their side of the water. Its sides were grey wooden panels that overlapped, and it bobbed and twisted, riding high and eager in the water. It was only a short distance upstream from the path, and Thither picked her way carefully along the bank edge until she got close.

"It is very small," she called back doubtfully. "And there is only one oar inside."

"Maybe we should look for a different way," Jericho replied, raising his voice over the sounds of the water.

Thither bit her lip and looked down at the boat, and then at Jericho.

"I want to try this," she called.

Jericho did not want to, but there was something in her voice, so he nodded and began walking up the bank. Seeing him coming, Thither turned and stepped into the small boat. As soon as she did, the boat stopped twisting and bouncing on the surface and turned downstream. The rope tying it to the pointed rock pulled taut, and then snapped.

"Thither!" Jericho shouted in shock and surprise.

Thither sat down hard in the boat and gripped both sides with white knuckles. The boat spun around in a fast eddy, and it seemed as if the stream surged with sudden whitecaps and spraying water. The girl gave a small whoop, whether of fear or surprise or something else Jericho could not tell, and her gaze locked on the stream in front of her. The trees leant down over the water, and their dark leaves began to shiver. To rustle, perhaps in excitement.

"Use the oar!" Jericho called out. "Reach out!"

The boat straightened and rushed downstream. Thither snatched up the oar and pushed it out, reaching towards him, and he saw it might work. Then her gaze turned back to that dark tunnel of stream, to the trees, to the water and forest.

Her face changed. The fear stayed, but something else rose—it might have almost been eagerness.

She dropped the oar.

As the boat rushed by, Thither spoke. Jericho could not hear the words over the water, but he felt them, because they were so full.

"For myself," she said. "By myself."

And then she was swept away, riding high in the little boat.

Jericho tried to follow the bank downstream, but as soon as he stepped off the path at the water's edge the trees crowded in close, pushing their trunks together, pushing their trunks at him, and shivering their leaves in an angry discordance. He thought about trying to wade through the shallow water, but when he got too close the edge gave way and the water rose up to gobble chunks of the bank right at his feet.

Thither was gone, and he was alone in the forest. He stepped back on the path, and when he did he saw he was on the far side of the stream. Or perhaps the stream had slipped away down the path behind him somehow. There was nothing stopping him from going on, and it might be that the stream would now stop him going back.

"Why?" he said aloud. He did not know exactly what he was asking, and he did not know the answer. He thought the word sounded empty. The yellow-haired man's words had been full when he fed the birds. Thither's words had been full enough that Jericho did not even need to hear them, when she was in the boat. But he did not know what that meant, and he did not know how to make his own words sound full.

Jericho ate an apple from his bag. He was not hungry, but holding the small red fruit in his hand reminded him of his mother. He wondered why he had wanted to come to the forest, and why the curse mattered. If the curse took people, if the forest took people, then it was only because those people went into the forest. Would the forest be safe if someone broke the curse?

Would the wider world be better off if it that happened?

Jericho started down the path again, and soon the stream was not even a murmuring behind him. He walked on, and the forest began to darken. The trees began to still their incessant shifting, and the sound of their leaves dropped to a lulling shush.

There was a light between the trees ahead, the flickering orange of firelight that made Jericho both eager and anxious. The trees drew apart and he stepped into a small clearing. There was no path leading away that he could see. There was a campfire in the middle of the space, burning low, and next to it, sitting on a small log, there was a woman in a simple dress. She turned as he came close, and the light flickered across her face in a way that made her look ancient and excited and young and tired and many other things.

"Hello," she said, and her voice was full.

"Hello," Jericho said. There was another small log nearby, little more than an old branch, and he sat himself down on it. He was tired. It had been a long day.

"Would you like an apple?" he asked the woman. "Or some bread?"

"No," she said, and smiled a little. "I don't need those things." Her voice was so full that Jericho wondered how he had ever been uncertain of hearing such.

They sat by the fire for a while, and the forest grew darker around them. Finally, the woman turned to Jericho, and her face was now more a mask of shadows than anything the fire could illuminate.

"Do you want to break the curse?"

"How would I do that?" Jericho replied. It was the question he had always been asking, even when he asked other questions.

"Here, now, you can have one thing that you want. You just need to ask," the woman replied, and even though he could not see it, he thought she might be smiling a little. "If ending the curse is that thing, you may have it. Is that what you want?"

He almost said yes straight away, but he thought he had heard something different in one of the woman's words. He thought of his day in the forest. He had seen a man finding importance in feeding small birds from his own hurt, and he had seen Thither ride the boat into the unknown by herself, for herself, sitting tall and eager with only her own choice for company. They had done those things, and their words had become full. He had not understood, but he had heard. He had listened, as his mother had told him.

He wondered if "curse" was an empty word, when the woman spoke it.

The fire crackled, the leaves whispered overhead, and the trees stirred sleepily. The woman waited, and Jericho tried to listen, finally, to the words deep inside himself.

"I do not want that," he said in the end, and he could hear the fullness of his own words. "I would like to go home."

A log broke in the small fire, and the orange light pushed the darkness back. The woman smiled. She was neither old nor young now, but Jericho thought it was a nice smile. An honest smile, if not an open one. She pointed, and even though the light was poor, he could see the thin path clearly on the far side of the clearing, where it had not been before.

"That path will take you home," she said. "As it did for your mother before you."

Familiar

Bernadette, my love,

I am writing this in your journal, using the blank pages at the back. I have not read what you have written. I will not invade your privacy like that.

My father sees me writing these human words and scowls. He does not understand. He wants me to go home, back to the scouring winds and curling baked earth, or he wants me to find another of your kind.

As if you could ever really be gone. As if you are like those little metal keys humans so often carry, that you think are important but so often misplace or forget.

Last night I travelled to the Estate of my father's human and watched them together. My father bowed low, his black horns almost touching the ground, and did as he was bid. He fed youth and vitality into his vain and stooped companion, and he smiled a little as the years of the mortal turned back. It was a smile of pride in a job well done, a smile of companionship built on a foundation of time, but it was as cold as our realm is hot. My father knows nothing of passion. He does not know you cannot be gone. You would not leave me like that.

Would you?

Awaiting your return,
Desi.

Bernadette,

Your world has always been cold, but it is colder now. You brought me here, to this unpleasant realm, and I stayed for you.

And still I stay. More than stay—today I went to a thing called "Orientation". A world of books and quiet contemplation was always your dream, not mine. You took my dream when you took yourself away. So I have decided to come to this place of learning, this place you talked of. I will take this dream of yours and you cannot stop me.

There was another of my kind in the group. Yes, we are rare, but I have heard we are more common now than in the times of ago, more plentiful than shown in the pages of story. That one had shimmery green skin and flicked their long tongue out as if they were tasting for danger.

They smiled at me and my horns crackled with my anger, my eyes seared with disgust. I wanted to burn them to a scaly crisp. I wanted to howl and scream and rent the air with the power I had given you, the power that had returned to me so suddenly. How dare they be here, free, their heart so much more than a black and gaping hole?

And how dare you? How DARE you? Do you not remember after that first incantation, when you breached the circle and placed your hand on mine? How we looked at each other in that moment, and you smiled? I could have destroyed you!

Instead I held your hand. And you destroy me.

Desirelda.

Berney,

Today I appeared before a human they name "Professor". He was a pale, hunched thing behind his giant desk. He peered at me through those thick glasses that some humans wear, as if such a paltry thing as eyesight could not simply be fixed for the asking.

"Oh, my," he said, but mildly. "These are not office hours."

"Are you the Professor of Comparative Magics? The one who knows of my kind? And of other non-human things?" I asked.

He was quiet a moment, and then pointed at a leather chair that might have held me. I did not sit.

"Do you know of a way to bring back the dead?" I asked.

The little wrinkled human looked surprised, and then sad. He shook his head slowly.

"I would give much," I said. And then, because it was true, "I would bind myself to you, if needed."

He adjusted his glasses, and the way he looked at me made my eyes sting. I was born of flame and smoke. I do not wish to know tears as I do.

"I think you are already bound," he said.

He was wise, and useless.

All I have is yours,

Desi.

Bernadette,

Today I sat in one of the classes you had seemed so eager for. My presence caused both glances and whispers, but not many. I counted four of my kind seated amongst the young humans. I saw the scaled one, and another with sharp feathers and a roving third eye.

Another had tall and twisted horns, although you would say they were not as resplendent as mine. Remember the night you told me they shimmered like they contained dark galaxies? I wonder, now, if you stared at them and saw too much. Reflected darkness, perhaps. I should have realised. Why did I not see beyond your smile, and your soft touch?

I should have wondered how someone could be so reckless, so daring as to bare themselves as you did. There may be an answer in your journal, if I could bring myself to turn the pages back. I will not. I cannot.

Your world is too cold.

I am sorry.

Desirelda.

My love,

You are gone. My father says there is indeed no crossing back, and I believe him. He does not know of all we had, but he sees much with those golden eyes.

He says going home will help. That the cracked and desiccated plains and the hot winds will scour me, cast me anew. That it will help me forget.

I will not go.

I will stay in your cold world, the world where you laid your soft hand on mine. The world where you breached the circle and gave up your safety with your small and reckless smile. I will think of all you gave me, and all I hoped I gave to you.

I will stay in the world in which I became—

Your Desi.

There Are Things On Me

I grit my teeth as I bump down the driveway, wincing as the underside of my car scrapes across rocks and dirt. The scene in front of me is all wrong. The place should be neat as a pin. Gran should be standing out on the trim green lawn, eager to usher me to the kitchen table, where she will fuss and click her tongue while Pop grumbles and spoons an absurd amount of sugar into his tea. Instead, the house slumps in on itself, a lumpy shadow under trees surrounded by unmanaged, weedy space. I can't see Gran or Pop anywhere.

I stop short of the turnaround, wary of the washed-out ruts that are likely hiding in the yellowing grass. I turn the car off and the frigid air I have been blasting dies a muggy, warm death. Even this late in the afternoon, the eucalypts leaning close to the house are exhausted, their leaves hanging limply in the last remnant of the day's heat. One has fallen against a wall, drunken and rotten. The grass in the yard is long and ragged and dying. The veranda is just a suggestion of wooden boards in the deep shadows, and the flyscreen door is hanging open, the doorway a black, gaping hole.

Something shifts beyond the threshold, and when I squint, I see someone. I think. I get out of my car, and the heat first runs its hot breath up and down my skin and then swallows me whole.

"Gran? Pop?" I call, as sweat beads on my neck and runs down the inside of my shirt. "Gran, is that you?"

Maybe I see more movement beyond the door, but I'm not sure. I pick my way through the tall grass, searching in vain for the path.

"Pop?"

As I put one foot on the grey, splintered veranda it gives slightly. The smell of rot and dark earth rises, hot and humid.

"Shit," I grunt, as I lose my balance and go down on one knee.

My hands slap the wood and the boards feel unpleasantly spongy. A thin grey figure appears in the doorway, framed in darkness.

"Come on, then," Pop says, his voice soft, and then he disappears into the dimness.

I stand in the doorway, peering into shadows. "God, Pop, open some curtains."

"Leave them," he says, his voice low and wet. He moves with the exaggerated care of someone who distrusts their own bones, and settles carefully into the tired recliner in front of the boxy old television.

It is marginally cooler inside, but it smells like that puff of air from under the veranda, thick and festering. I move slowly as my eyes adjust.

"Is everything okay?" I ask, even though everything is obviously not.

Pop isn't okay either. He was never a big man, but he used to have the wiry, knotted appearance that takes some small men as they age. Now, his face is too thin, his cheeks empty and sagging, and his skin is too grey, even in the shadows of the room. He is shrinking, collapsing in on himself as if in sympathy with the failing house that surrounds him. My guilt rises up, as cloying as the air in the room. I live far away, but I should have come sooner. More often.

He doesn't answer, but I can hear him breathing. He pulls at the air with a faint gurgling effort.

"Pop," I say gently as I kneel by him. "You don't sound well."

"Fine," he says. "We are…I am fine."

His breath on my face is too warm, and I try not to pull away from the wet earthiness of it.

"Where's Gran?"

His eyes, too dark and too large, roll towards me and then

away. "Sick," he says, and then coughs. "In bed." He shifts and moves absently, rubbing at his arms.

The voice is high and querulous, but bubbly as well. "Is someone here?"

Gran is standing in the bedroom doorway. I am too shocked to speak. Her nightgown hangs off her, and her skull looks both bulbous and too heavy on her thin neck. She takes a step forward, and turns her head this way and that, the shadows covering her features.

"I can hear them again," she mutters.

"It's me, Gran," I say, standing up.

She keeps swivelling her head back and forth. Then she takes another step forward and I can see her more clearly. Her hands move incessantly, feverishly, and when I look down I almost gag. She is scratching at her own arms with her long, bony fingers, and both of her stick-thin forearms are split and torn, weeping blood.

"There are things on me," she whispers, and she rolls her yellowed eyes around the dark room. "Things in me."

"I'm taking you both into town," I say as I wipe Gran's arms with the cleanest cloth I can find. I've also found an old tube of antiseptic and some oversized plaster dressings, and the scratches look like almost nothing by the time I'm done. When I finish, she is staring at me, eyes glazed. Her breath on my face is as hot as the sullen air outside.

"Into town? No," Pop says from the recliner, his voice so liquid it almost gurgles as he stares at the dead television screen.

"Pop," I say. "Look at this place." I gesture around the room pointedly, at the drawn curtains, the blank TV. "Look at you. Look at Gran. What does she mean? What does she think is on her?" *In her*, I don't say. I can't bring myself to say that.

Gran moans.

"Neither of you are well," I say. "And the house—"

"Shh!" Gran interrupts. "Can you hear them?" She cocks her head, and her eyes are suddenly bright.

"Hear what?" I ask. There is nothing beyond the quiet ticking of the corrugated iron roof cooling slightly, and my grandparents' wet breathing.

"Look—" I begin.

"Hush!" Pop says without looking around. He also seems to be listening to something that is not there.

"I'm going to call the doctor," I say. "Tell him I'm bringing you both in."

Neither of them reply straight away. For just a moment, a slight rustling rises all around, the sound of things moving in the dimness, there and then gone. The air itself seems to press close, to rub against my skin in feather-light touches, and I shudder and glance around. I see shadows and neglect and my own guilt staring at me from every dark corner. Gran is listening intently. I strain, but now there is nothing.

"There are things in me," Gran whispers. "Can you hear them?"

I gawk at her, unsure of what to say. The silence stretches out, full and heavy. Finally, Pop speaks.

"Too late to leave now," he says, so softly I almost don't catch it. "It's almost dark."

"Tomorrow then?" I ask.

He nods, and Gran nods faintly as well.

I hesitate. There is something very wrong with Gran. Pop doesn't seem much better. But I don't know how I would get them into the car if they refused, short of dragging them both. I nod. Tomorrow will be soon enough.

The setting sun bleeds orange through the kitchen window. I've tried the lights but they don't work, and the shadows are growing towards me from the corners of the room. For just a moment I think there is a faint rustling sound again, and then I hear a shuffling step behind me.

Pop is standing just beyond the kitchen door, back in the dark.

"You should not have come," he says, and then draws another struggling breath.

"Are you kidding?" I say, and my anger at myself sharpens my words. "Why didn't you tell me things were like this? What happened to the electricity?"

I step towards him, my anger growing. Pop is sick. Gran is sicker. He should have done something. I should have.

He shifts back as if he doesn't want me too close. The last of the sunlight briefly washes his arms in dark orange. He is rubbing at them again. As he does, I think I glimpse, just for a moment, small movements under the skin. Tiny lumps, shifting this way and that.

"What...?"

I take another step forward, but there is nothing to see.

Pop breathes wetly for a second before speaking. "Too late now. Dark soon."

I swallow my anger with some difficulty. Tomorrow I will get them into town and away from here.

***

I flick on the light in the spare room and nothing happens, of course.

"No light," Pop mutters from behind me.

The room is hot and smells thick with dust. The bed is barely a grey outline now the sun has set. I fumble my phone out and turn on the flashlight.

Pop grunts and shifts back into the hallway. I barely notice, given what I am looking at in the bright white illuminated circle.

"What the..."

The corner of the room is a huge, misshapen brown pillar. It spreads across the floor and rises up to the ceiling, across the ceiling, tendrils of brown material wending outwards and plunging behind the panelling, as if burrowing into the struts and supports that make up the bones of the place. In the middle it bulges out, like it has paused in the act of bubbling across the room. Half of the bedside table has been consumed, and what is left is split and rotten.

"Is...is that a termite nest?" I ask, but there is no answer.

Pop is gone. I don't need an answer anyway. That first stab of light from my phone has shown more than the dark spreading trunk and tendrils. The brown surface is dotted with hundreds, maybe thousands, of small, moving white bodies. They scurry frantically away from the light, and a sound rises from in front of me, from behind, from all around. A rustling—no, more like whispers.

"Gran?" I call. "Pop?"

There's no answer. The rustling sound stops when I speak, and a silence falls, heavy and full. The termites stop as well, all of them, all at once. They should be rushing away from the light, but they are just…still. I think of Gran and Pop, going still, listening.

Gran and Pop in this house, sitting in the dark with this *thing*.

I turn towards the hallway, to get to them, to get out of here, and the floor that seemed solid enough a minute ago now sags underneath me, like on the veranda. Momentum keeps me moving, and my next step sends my foot straight through the boards. I throw my hands out in front of me as I fall and my phone goes flying, the light flashing across the walls as the thing clatters into the hallway. The space underneath the floor is deep, and I drop in up to my thigh. My other leg twists out painfully behind me. The broken edges of the wooden boards dig through my pants and into the muscle underneath.

"Fuck!"

I pull myself forward and the floor sags further but holds. I roll onto my back and put my hand to my leg. It comes away wet—I'm bleeding. Bleeding and laying on the rotten floor in the dark.

"Gran! Pop!" I call, but there is no answer.

It's too dark. I put my hand back to my leg. There is blood, but it doesn't feel like much. A scratch, really. But then something runs across my hand. Some*things*. Lots of them, light touches as whatever they are run up my wrist and forearm. The scent of wet rot fills my nose and my mind. I can't see all those eerily still termites in the dark, but I can guess they are not still anymore.

I haul myself up, trying not to gag, and focus on the circle of light from my phone in the hallway. I limp out to it, shaking my hands and brushing them up and down my arms, trying to get the damn crawling things off me. Trying to stop those insistent touches. Trying to brush away the sweet, sickly smell of decay. There must be hundreds of them. They creep over my shoulders, under my shirt, across my stomach.

I snatch up my phone. The light jitters and jumps across my front, my legs. I am covered in the tiny white creatures. My arms are smeared with wet, pasty remains where I have squashed them in my frantic brushing, but there are so many more, crawling all over me. I yell and brush at them with one hand as I stumble down the hall and towards the front room, holding my phone out in front of me. There are feathery touches up my neck, and that rustling sound comes back, rising and falling like whispers.

"Gran!" I scream as I hold my phone up in front of me. "Pop!"

Pop is sitting in his recliner. He is scratching frantically at both of his arms, the skin of his forearms torn and bloody. He rolls his eyes in the flickering white light.

"There are things," he moans. "Things on me. In me."

I shriek and turn, even as the tickling sensation reaches my ears. The rustling rises again. My phone light washes across the walls, pushing feebly at the shadows.

Gran is standing in her bedroom doorway. She takes a step forward, and it looks as if her head is more bulbous than before, swollen and misshapen. Her arms hang in bloody tatters by her sides.

Something tickles at my ears, and inside my ears, and the rustling becomes louder.

Gran falls forward. She makes no effort to catch herself, and her head hits the floor with a soft, ripe sound. She lays still, the pale light from my phone reflected in her staring eyes as I shout her name. Termites are streaming from her ears, her nose, her mouth, and I realise dimly that I am brushing frantically at my neck and my ears with my free hand even as I stand there. Those light, feathery touches move into my ears, into my head, caressing, feeling, *burrowing*. The whispering builds until it is everything. I think I might be screaming now, but I can't hear it. There is just darkness, and that whispering.

The curtains are drawn against the heat of the day, against the terrible light of the sun, and the room is dark. Pop is in his chair but he is so very still now, as still as Gran. My breath bubbles, as if my throat is full of something. The rustling, the whispering is all around and inside my head. I sit on the floor and scratch at my arms. Things run across my skin, even though I cannot see them.

There are things on me. There are things in me.

The Taste Of Immolation

The blistered tip of my finger is white and shrivelled at the edges. It throbs—a tiny heartbeat, a shard of pulsing mirror. I place it in my mouth, as I did when I was an innocent, when I touched the hot thing and first learned of that type of hurt.

The stovetop is as red now as it was all those years ago. The tip of my finger is warm with pain, and bitter. It tastes almost like a remembering. Almost.

The skin of my finger is flat and grey and dead. There is no heartbeat now, no memory. And yet it must still be there.
Somewhere.
Deeper.
When the stovetop reddens, I hold my finger to it again. I can smell the dead skin burn. It means nothing, this burning away of what was a part of me, but then the raw flesh awakens. I hold it there a moment longer, and when I lift it there is a *pulling* sensation as that small part of me is left on the red surface of the burner. The small circle of meat I have given up blackens and shrivels even as I put my finger in my mouth again.

It is not warm now. It is hot, and the hard wet ridges at the top of my mouth echo the burning heat as I touch them. The taste returns, stronger—the taste of more than just my pain, the echo of something forgotten. Something that burned. Something *I* burned.

There is something white and hard amidst the cracked and weeping ruin of my fingertip. Bone is not what I seek. Memory is buried deeper than bone. It is buried under pain.

My charred flesh throbs anew each time I return it to the stovetop, and in the end it screams. Parts of my tongue and the roof of my mouth have blistered and peeled, and the taste is very strong. Something stirs within me, shapes beyond the pain, shapes that I made. But still it is not enough. I cannot see.

My hand is a curled and blackened thing, dripping blood that sizzles on the burner. The inside of my mouth is nothing but puckered and sour strips. It tastes like shame.

I am close. There is a white wall of soundless screaming inside that is my pain but also something that *was*, and I tremble with exertion, with agony, with realisation.

With responsibility.

I am *so* close. There are charred and blackened bodies in my mind, in my memory, but I cannot see them clearly. Not quite.

I lower my mouth to the red surface.

Death Meets Noel Samuelson

The first time Death meets Noel Samuelson is in the sunny back yard of the boy's family home. Noel looks up at Death with tears in his pale blue eyes. He is holding Bozo, the old grey-muzzled terrier.

"He won't wake up," the boy says. His voice is very small.

"No," Death replies. "He won't."

Death doesn't talk to many people. Death exists in those moments of stillness that mark the ending of a life, and it is quite rare for someone living to make an appearance. Sometimes Death thinks it might be nice if it happened a little more often.

The boy starts to sob, hard, his little body shaking, and Death pulls their robe up above their knobbly knees and squats down on the grass. They reach out to the dog but stop short of touching him with their thin, grey fingers.

"Bozo. Thirteen years, two months and sixteen days. Died of an aneurysm while dreaming of barking at a flock of geese," Death says. Death knows about endings. They look at Noel, but Noel does not seem to have heard through all the tears.

"It was a good way to die," Death says.

"He was such a good dog," Noel says, without looking up.

Death does not know about that. They don't know anything about life, or the living.

Instead of replying they reach out again and this time they touch the dog. Pet the dog, really, stroking the back of Bozo's neck softly. A soft light appears and coalesces into a small shape—a patchwork of thin metal pieces like tin, welded together into a stylised heart. There is a small key sticking out of it—a toy key, almost, but one that looks dull and worn. Both of these things are new to Death, but the key feels familiar. Death pulls it out. In it they can feel the end of Bozo. There is an echo of geese and excited barking, and then a large amount of nothing. Noel stares at Death, and at the heart.

"He is dead," Death says—and because the key is something moulded by Noel's presence—"his key has stopped turning."

Death stands up and brushes their robes down absently. This frozen image of the back yard is fading, and it is time for Noel to fade as well, back into life. Whatever that is.

The second time they meet, Death is almost pleased. Something about the blue-eyed boy has gotten under Death's skin. It itches.

Now the boy is a blue-eyed man. Death looks up from the bicycle and the young woman in the street to see Noel standing on the sidewalk. Noel steps gingerly forwards, no doubt unaware he is now outside of his life and not really in the street at all.

There is blood on the asphalt, but it does not flow in this snapshot that is a life ended. Noel stops at the edge of the unmoving redness.

"Hello again," he says. "I wondered if you were real. With Bozo." He looks down at the unmoving cyclist, his face a little pale. "I didn't see what happened to her."

Death looks down as well. "Her name was Michelle. It wasn't her fault. The driver didn't notice the red light." They pause, and then, because they are not great at conversation, "Twenty three, three months and nineteen days."

"Oh," says Noel. "Are you going to do the key thing again?"

It is not common for someone to fall into another's moment of Death, and Noel has done it twice now. Death cannot recall that happening before.

But Michelle's moment needs to be dealt with, and Noel is watching with interest. Death bends down and places two of their long, too-thin fingers on Michelle's cheek.

The light coalesces and a small, tinny heart appears. This one is a little more dented than Bozo's, but essentially the same. A little key has appeared as well, and Death plucks it from the heart. There is the sound of car tires, and screaming, and a flash of panic. And then nothing. Like always.

"It must be hard, doing this all the time," Noel says quietly.

Death thinks of all that nothing. There has been quite a lot of it.

"Why a tin heart?" Noel asks.

Death shrugs. "You see what you see." Usually they deal in impressions, in the abstract, when there is no mortal about. Death only sees the heart, and the key, because Noel does. "It is the key that is important," they continue. "I only deal in endings, and the key holds the ending." Death can feel that.

"Then why is there a heart?"

Death does not answer. This moment is over. It was nice to have someone to share it with, but there is work to do. Yet, as the frozen stillness of the ending fades and Noel begins to fade as well, Death realises what that itch is about. They turn back.

"I can't see your end," Death says. They know Noel's name but nothing else. That has never happened before. But Noel has already gone, and all that is left is the useless heart sitting on the road.

The third time they meet, Noel is sitting in a hard plastic chair, his wrinkled, age-spotted hands clasped tightly in front of him. Next to him, in bed, is a small woman with white frizzy hair. Irene Samuelson, seventy two years, one month and three days, multiple organ failure due to late-stage pancreatic cancer.

Noel looks up and gives Death a tiny, shaky smile.

"I thought I might see you," he says. His voice is small, like it was the first time they met.

Death has been thinking about Noel. Death wonders if they have maybe pulled Noel into this moment, with all that thinking.

"Hello," Death says, trying not to sound uncertain. Death should not be uncertain.

Noel places a hand on his wife's wrist. "Was she in pain, these last few days?"

"I don't know," Death says, shifting a little. "That was life. I don't know about life."

The frozen moment that is the end of Irene stretches out.

"Will you do the key thing?" Noel finally asks.

In response, Death reaches out. They touch Irene's thin, almost translucent skin, and the light draws together just above the bedsheets.

And then Noel reaches across and grabs Death's hand. Death gasps, too shocked to try to pull away. No one has ever touched them before. The light brightens and focuses, and then there are suddenly two small tin hearts sitting on the bed. Irene's is dark and dented, and the key is a sad, blackened thing. The other heart has not fared much better, but both it and the key still glint with a few patches of clean, shiny metal. Death stares. The second key is turning.

Noel pulls the blackened key from Irene's heart, and then he lets go of Death's hand and grabs his own key.

"Don't—" Death starts, reaching out. As they do, their hand brushes against Noel's tin heart.

In that touch, Death feels something.

Something new.

It is strong. It is something from Noel, something *of* Noel. Something of the years in between this eternity of frozen moments. There is laughter and tears and boredom and haste. A crying boy. A dead terrier. An accident, and a tall, hooded figure standing in the street, their feet in frozen blood. A young man, clumsy and blushing, and a smiling woman with frizzy hair. There is office work and stress and the grinding of seconds and minutes and hours, and there is the soft feel of lips on skin. Death does not know about life, but this heart is a roiling mess of it.

It comes all in a moment, and Death gasps and staggers a little. It is so much. It is just a glimpse. They can feel it, so much, churning inside them now.

Noel pulls his own key out and jams it into the worn tin heart of his wife. The key shudders for a moment, and then starts to turn. His wife draws a long, shaky breath and then fades away, gone from this frozen moment. Gone back to life.

Noel looks at the small blackened key that was his wife's, and then holds it out.

"Sorry," Noel says, but Death thinks he is not really sorry. There was so much in the heart, so much behind that simple action of swapping the keys, but nothing that would make Noel regret what he just did.

Death takes the key. In it, they can feel an end, but it is not Irene's. Now there is a different feel to it, a shape that matches the life of Noel.

"Noel Samuelson," Death says. "Seventy-three years, two months, three days. Died giving his wife some more time." Death hears their own voice catch a little. They weigh the key in their hand, weigh the ending, and the nothing that is behind it, that will follow it. Death regards Noel, this small man who sobbed so over his dog just moments ago, so long ago. And Death looks at the battered heart, the small tin shape that still has a bit of shine left to it.

Death bends and pushes the key into the heart, giving it a few quick twists. They have never done anything like this before, and are surprised at how easy it is. As they straighten, they feel again the laughter, the tears, and the years of hurt and hope that Noel has already had.

Noel fades from view, the little man's mouth open as if he is trying to say something. Death hears nothing, but it does not matter. They can wait to see Noel for a fourth time. It will only be a moment or two, after all.

Sleep, Empty

I dream of falling.

There is fear as the air rushes by, and surrender tinted with the darkest exhilaration. There may be an end, and there may have been a beginning, but for now there is only the falling. It fills me.

And then I jerk awake in the dark. For a moment I still hear the roar of the air, and the thud of my heart throwing itself against its cage. I grip the edges of my bed. It was only a dream.

The thudding fades, and as the dream recedes a little as well and the lethargy of interrupted sleep floods in, there is another sound. It takes longer than it should to place it, here on the edge of waking and in the slowest part of night.

There is someone at the door.

The apartment is full of dark outlines and contrary memories, and I bark my shin on the side table and stub my toe on something hard before I even think to turn on a light. The knocking comes again, slow, deliberate, at odds with the early hour. It is too loud, a sharp shock running through the building's quiet.

I don't expect anything good. Half-awake though I am, I still remember to very quietly place my eye to the peephole. I am still fuzzy, and now my toe is throbbing, but I recognise my visitor. Old Mrs Swainson from down the hall is no threat. There must be something wrong. I open the door and blink against the harsh corridor light.

My neighbour does not say anything. She is tiny, a diminutive shape almost lost inside her grey robe, and she is wearing pink hippopotamus-shaped slippers. Her hair is a halo of grey frizz.

"Are you okay, Mrs Swainson?" I ask, my voice a little croaky. I am still trying to shake off that feeling of falling.

She is staring upwards. The lights overhead are bright, and I can hear a slight buzzing, one of those low sounds that slinks out and takes over such spaces in quiet times. I squint up as well, and then around at nothing, and then back at her. She lowers her face, very slowly, until she is looking right at me.

I almost step back and close the door in one sweeping motion. I stop myself, though. Mrs Swainson is old, and confused, and she is standing in the corridor in her robe and ridiculous slippers. And despite what I see, I like her. I always have. She always seemed like she had weathered the years of apartment building living without becoming too hard or too brittle, or too strange. Until now.

Her eyes are a mess, now that I see them properly. They are badly bloodshot, and so sunken that the skin underneath them is a horrible soft purple. The skin around them has sagged as well, and her gaze is hot, as if she is so full of fever it is melting her face. I have never seen someone so tired.

"You have them, Gary," she says. "You are full of them." She sways a little as she speaks. Her voice is soft and she looks around again, her eyes lingering on the walls, the floor, the hall.

"What?" I ask. My hand tightens on the door frame.

"Can I have them?" Mrs Swainson asks, suddenly focussing on me again, her sagging features intense.

"Have what?" I ask on reflex. And then, "Are you okay? Can I call someone?"

"Your dreams," Mrs Swainson says, leaning forward as she does. "Can I have them?"

I pull away. I should close the door. Or I should call someone. I should do *something*.

She pulls back slightly at my movement, and then starts to cry softly, her head hanging low. She makes a little whining noise as well, that at first I think is part of the buzzing of the lights. The sounds overlap in my head, the buzzing and the whining.

"Hey," I say, not wanting to say anything, not wanting to be there at all, but not knowing what else to do. "Hey, you can.

Sure you can." It is nonsense, this is all nonsense and maybe worse, maybe an old lady losing her mind, but as I speak I think of that falling dream. I have others, sure I do, just like everyone, fragments and oh-so-real scenes and trumpeting sequences of both high embarrassment and desire, but the falling one I hate.

As soon as I speak she stops crying. She looks up at me, but she doesn't smile. Her sunken, dark eyes are steady in her sagging, melting face. The buzz of the lights is low and insistent. She doesn't look crazy or muddled now. She just looks tired.

"I'm sorry," she says. She starts to shuffle backwards. "I'm sorry."

I am exhausted. I stop at the little café on the corner like usual, but today I ask for a double espresso, even though I think maybe it won't help. I drink it quickly, my mind full of the night before. The hours after Mrs Swainson's appearance had been, strangely, the best sleep I had in a long, long time—deep and dark and overflowing with nothing. And yet I am exhausted.

It is a thing to think about, as I drink my bitter coffee and walk the middling distance to work. Sometimes my early hours are broken and restless, my mind pushing itself away from dream fragments and towards waking worry. It is a malady I am sure I share with many, but the hours after Mrs Swainson's visit had been different. I do not ascribe those few hours of dreamless slumber to the old lady's odd request—of course not, although there is always something to be said for suggestion, or self-suggestion. But even so, last night, when I should have been restless, disturbed by Mrs Swainson's sagging, haggard face or the image of her shuffling off down the corridor in her ridiculous slippers, I had slept. It had been as still and empty as bottomless, lightless water, but it had not refreshed. Instead, I am so very, very tired. I think again of Mrs Swainson, her sunken and bruised eyes, and the sagging skin of her face as the lights buzzed overhead.

The espresso does not help.

I leave work early—I am too tired to crunch numbers. Adding digits, even using the fill function in the spreadsheet, is too much on top of the Herculean effort of keeping my eyes open. The only thing that stops me dozing is the image of Swainson with her drooping, aged face and her quiet crying as she stands in the hallway. I can't stop seeing her. I can't stop hearing her.

I am walking slowly down the street when I realise I am cold. I have been cold for several blocks, actually, but I have forgotten my jacket—maybe at work, although I cannot recall. I hug myself but I do not turn back. The cold has worked its way into my brain, and for a moment I am feeling more than half there, almost awake. I slip into a convenience store and buy a piping hot black coffee. As I stand near the machine, sipping it, breathing the bitterness in deep, I hear the door open and someone come in.

"Can I have them?" a voice asks, and I take a large gulp of my coffee in surprise. It burns, but the pain brings focus, cutting through the remaining fog in my head.

There is a reply, something from the cashier that I don't catch, although the tone is dismissive. I take the few steps towards the counter needed to clear my view.

It is not Mrs Swainson. Of course not. There is a young man standing at the counter, leaning on the counter, pressing into it, really. All I can see is the back of a dirty denim jacket and untidy brown hair. Despite the chill outside, I can smell the man, drying rancid sweat mixed with the bitter aroma of the brew in my hand.

"You are so full," the leaning man whines, and my hand shakes so hard I spill hot coffee on my wrist.

"Get out of here!" the cashier yells. He is young, too, brown-skinned and wide eyed, a thread of panic running his words together. "I'm sick of this! I'll call the cops! Go!"

The young man leaning on the counter rights himself very slowly, as if he is trying to remember how to move. He turns. He is thin, and very pale, and his eyes are sunken and dark. There is dirt on his face. He pivots his head slowly, left and right, before settling on me. He looks confused.

"Empty," he says absently, and shuffles to the door.

I stare at the closing door, the coffee cooling in my mouth, and then I turn back to the cashier.

"That's the third one today," the cashier says, a tremble in his voice.

I don't register the words properly. For a moment I don't feel tired, I don't feel slow or foggy at all. The sight of the cashier cuts through my dazed mind. I stare, and the cashier stares back, suddenly wary. They are so real, so vibrant, so…*full*. That's the word. I take a step forward. I swallow and open my mouth, and then I realise what I am about to say. To ask.

I leave instead, in a shuffle that feels like a run. It is far harder than it should be not to look back at the cashier as I go.

"**G**ary. Gary!"

The voice cuts through the fog and I jerk upright. I have a moment of utter confusion as I stare at my work desk. The bright computer screen is filled with a spreadsheet that screams in bright white, and the little mug I put my pencils in exists at the far end of a lengthening, gyrating tunnel. Perhaps it is the cashier speaking. Maybe I am in the convenience store. I look around blearily.

"Earth to Gary!" a voice says. A chipper, happy, grating voice.

"Huh?" I ask the world in general. I don't remember the evening after the convenience store. I don't remember getting to work again, on what seems to be another day. I don't recall working, either, although the glaring spreadsheet is half done. I think of pink slippers, shaped like hippos. Of cashiers, and the smell of drying sweat.

"Are you okay?" the voice asks—just like I had asked Mrs Swainson. I turn, and the world of the office revolves slowly around me, some sort of slow, vertiginous ride I had not meant to get on. I have always hated that loopy, loose feeling of coasters and tilt-a-whirls. That feeling of disconnect, of no control. Almost like falling. Almost like a dream.

A face appears. Pale, narrow features framed by red hair, all of it floating above a sensible grey knee-length dress. The face frowns and looms over me, swelling to fill my vision, and then pulling back. I stare, unable to think of what else to do.

"Marcy?" I ask, finally. My tongue is thick.

"Are you okay, Gary?" The woman's eyes flick to my screen. "In the zone, eh?"

My brain, swinging on a pendulum, cresting a ride. My brain, falling.

She frowns at me.

"Are you okay?" she asks again. "You look tired."

"Yeah," I say as the room finally steadies and Marcy's face stops lurching towards me. "Bad dreams."

I don't know why I said that. I don't really know Marcy. Or maybe I do. I'm not sure. I could have easily said I didn't sleep well, but that is not true—I have been sleeping deeply, sleeping without dreams. Maybe. My mind is so foggy. There was a cashier. A woman in pink slippers. Buzzing lights. I remember surfacing from somewhere deep, waking slowly to bright morning light. Surfacing unsatisfied. Empty.

Marcy nods, and her red hair shifts and sways. I blink slowly. She is so real. So *there*. I think of the cashier. Vibrant. Full.

"What are you trying to work through?" She grins as she says it, and I try to parse her words. Maybe a joke. I don't get it, but I'm not sure if it is my grogginess or just the strangeness of words falling from one person towards another. Such a strange thing, words. Pieces of thought, broken.

"You know what I mean," she continues. Now she is frowning a little, and I wonder if I have done something wrong. "Dreams are a way of processing things. A reset, kind of. Your brain, sifting out detritus, getting you ready for the next round. That's what they say, anyway."

"Oh," I say. I think of Swainson. Is that who this woman means when she says *they*? A *they* who knows about dreams. "Sometimes I dream of falling."

"We all have that one, Gary." The woman, Marcy—I think maybe that is her name—shrugs and turns to go. I watch her. Yes, she must have dreams, I am sure—she is so *full*.

I want to ask, but she is gone.

I wake in the dark. I reach out for the light by my bed, but my hand finds nothing. I try to breathe and can't remember what that is. The world is gone, flooded by a spinning, empty blackness within which float small, shining pieces. A cashier looks at me in near-panic. Pink slippers step under buzzing lights. A red-headed woman looms in front of me, talking of falling, talking of dreams. She is so full, so full, and it is not fair.

I sit up—no, I am already sitting up. I breathe, finally. I do not know where I am. My mind fumbles, useless. The darkness stretches out and all around.

I must have slept, I should sleep, but it is so empty there. I close my eyes.

The light burns, and I groan. My eyes are so heavy. I force them open, and the world tilts around me. I bend forward, grasping the edges of the couch. It is morning already, and I am sweating through my clothes, drenched in my own reek from the day before. Next to me is a half empty container of congealed Thai food. My eyes are gummy, and when I stand the world tilts even more, threatening to slide away. All I want is rest, but my sleep is deep and dark and empty, and not anything that can help. I am so empty, and I need to be full. The cashier was full. Marcy was full.

I am in the lobby of my building.

I am on the street.

I am at an intersection. There is a steaming cup of coffee in my hand, but as I raise it to my lips the world spins and swoops away like a bird, like the wind. Like a dream. The cup falls to the ground, and the dull brown liquid runs across the concrete.

"Can I have them?" I hear, for the first time, for the thousandth time. It takes a second, it takes forever, to raise my head and look towards the voice. It is like falling, but I am still. There is a woman, a woman in a business suit, her hair blowing about, strands flailing for purchase against nothing. Her face has melted—no, her face sags, tired and purplish under her red eyes. She is talking to a teenage girl.

"Please?" she asks. Pleads.

The teenage girl laughs and spins away, spins and falls across the intersection without falling, a graceful, impossible dance.

"God, today is full of weirdos!" the girl laughs to images of herself that are all about her, fractured reflections moving in unison, moving away. I see their faces as they go, mocking, frightened, spinning smiles and screams and frowns. The girl is so full. Her swooping, mocking, fearful friends are so full. The business lady does not move. The business lady is empty, and weeping.

I look down at my spilt coffee. The world of the footpath becomes a hollow, twisting tunnel. People lurch towards and away from me. Words and faces, looping around me as I walk. They are all so full. They should share.

Marcy is screaming, and someone is pulling at me. I wonder if this is a dream, but no, Marcy has the dreams. She won't share. She is crying, and someone is holding me, and I am asking and asking. There is a whining, a pleading, and it sounds like buzzing lights. It sounds like Mrs Swainson. It sounds like me.

"Can I have them? Your dreams, can I have them?"

No one answers, but they grab and hold and spin me. It is sickening. They are forcing me to be empty. I pull away.

My shirt is torn, and the wind is cold. There is knocking. A knocking at my door—no, a banging, a banging like my door is metal. The world spins and slides as I look behind me. There are people, people coming out of the door onto the roof. Spilling out, milling, staring at me. I am on a roof. This must be a dream. I feel tears on my face, tears tracking over the sunken, sagging skin under my eyes. It *is* a dream. I have found a dream, finally. I look down at the edge of the roof, the edge just under my feet, and I smile. A dream of falling. This is it. I can be full again. I step forward.

A nd I dream of falling.

The Past Laid Out On The Table

The sky above his mother's house is the bright orange and pink of a frozen dawn when David stops by after work.

"Mum!" he yells as he slings the grocery bags at the kitchen bench. They slow to a stop in mid-air. A yellow lemon drops out of one bag and spins lazily, nowhere to go. No *when* to go.

"Yes, dear?"

"Have you looked out the window?" David says, trying to keep the edge from his voice. He wishes she would just leave the past alone.

"Oh, I'll put it all back," she says, and of course she will. She was always good like that. Always the ordered one. Always the careful one.

"Do you have time for a cup of tea?" she asks.

He wants to say no. He doesn't want to be here while she dips into the past again. He wants to say he is too busy, that he has his own family now and doesn't have time for this, that he won't have his own kids wondering for one second where he might be. But none of that really holds when time itself in the kitchen is so fractured, so broken into pieces that even the sky overhead is still stuck hours in the past.

"Okay then."

There are memories strewn across the kitchen table. He tries not to look, but some are just snippets—really nothing more than harmless little things. There is Horatio the teddy, brown and fuzzy and beady eyed, and there is his first pair of sneakers, ridiculous and tiny. Both of these things are impossibly new and so very *there*, plucked fresh from almost three decades before. Nearby, deep and dark but polished by so much handling, is the time his father carried his half-sleeping form from the car after late night basketball, his mother tiptoeing by their side. David looks away from that one, swallowing, trying not to remember those arms holding him. Trying not to imagine what either of his own children would think, if that comfort and safety was suddenly gone forever, with no explanation, no hint as to why. He blinks quickly. There is something hard in his chest.

He sits at the kitchen bench with his back to the table and focuses on his mother. She takes the kettle and pushes it forward a few minutes, just until the water is boiling. She can't do big objects, not like Dad could, but she is very good with the small stuff. She reaches up to the cupboard and back thirty years to where her favourite teacups are still bright and new. And yet, despite the deep blue rims and shiny white sides, one has a chip on the edge.

"Why don't you ever go back a little further? To when that cup wasn't chipped?"

"Oh, you know," she says as she hands him his tea. He doesn't know.

"Why do you keep doing this?" he asks.

"Doing what, dear?"

"Breaking things down into all these moments. Going back over the past. Pulling out mementos. I mean, Dad could never help fiddling with things, and look what happened."

She puts down her cup and looks at him, suddenly serious. "And what is it that happened, exactly?"

"Well, we don't know, do we? But does it matter? He left us, somehow, some when. It's not like he's popping up in any of these pieces you like to play with. Not like he just got himself stuck somewhere."

His mother looks down, her hands gripping her cup much too tightly. He hopes she won't break it. It would be hard to put something so delicate, from so long ago, back together.

"Is that it, Mum?" he asks, his voice low. "Are you still looking for him?"

"No, dear," she says softly. "He was always so much better at this than me. I know you are angry with him, but if he was still able to, he would be back. Or he would at least be there in one of our favourites, maybe just needing a little help. But every place, every time I check, he's not. I mean, of course he is, but he also isn't. Not in any of them. No, I'm not looking for him anymore."

Despite everything, David lets himself feel the pieces she has scattered about. Once he drops his guard, they pull at him, insistent. All that time, all those places. The newly handled, the too often handled, both the raw and the worn. Some of them deep and full of want. Full of need. Full of love. He can see her, and him, and them, their little family. Dad, laughing as he holds up David's first day of school for them all to see. David, bringing home a summer afternoon full of the flash of dragonflies above the little creek behind the house. His mother, taking a pleasant afternoon in the yard and stretching it out, and out, and out, while neither he nor his father really noticed. There is so much there, and so much lost.

"Why do you do it, then? Why do you keep doing it? It's all broken," David says, his voice rough. He didn't need this. He didn't need to see these things again, feel these things again. He has his own family now. He doesn't need to be pulled at like this. He doesn't want to be reminded of how close everything might be to breaking, no matter how strong, how right things might feel. He looks down at his now blurry teacup and almost pushes the tears back a few moments. Instead, he lets them fall. That hard thing in his chest is shifting.

His mother touches the chip on the edge of the teacup lightly.

"Remember?" she asks, and before he can answer she holds up the piece of the past she is talking about. In it he is small, and she is smiling at him. She is wiping away his tears, and pushing her teacup back a few minutes, to the moment that clumsy, excitable little David had dropped it. She can fix things, is fixing things, and yet she stops before the cup is quite whole. Stops while there is still one chip missing from the rim. Stops, because for her, the chip is more than a chip.

David closes his eyes. He sees the broken cup, and his own

tears. He sees his father laughing, holding up that first day of school. His father, carrying him, almost sleeping, from the car. His father, who he has never talked about to his own children. Dad, there and then gone, gone with no explanation or warning, and yet still there—always there, David realises. The hard thing in his chest comes loose and he cries out, reaching blindly for what was.

His mother catches his hands and holds them tight. David shakes and sobs and feels the past. The want. The need. The love. Slowly, his mother lets go and softly wipes away his tears, just as she had all that time ago.

"Sometimes the broken things are worth keeping too," she says.

Drowning In The Dark

1

I killed my brother when I was twelve years old.

There's some other stuff to start with. A lot of things are close to a story when you lay them down, but close is not a bill paid. That one's from my father. Funny how some things don't fade. I suspect I will always hear certain things in his tired voice, trying for levity but tinged with bitterness.

My father was an accountant. A successful one, too, despite Cooing being a pretty small place, and despite the two boys that chewed away his widower days like starving white ants. My earliest memories are of him in the kitchen impatiently packing lunches and spilling cereal.

"We've got to get up earlier," he would mutter, frowning. Or maybe it was "Fuck, no cornflakes." Or sometimes "Caleb, for God's sake get your brother up."

Mikey was a couple of years older than me, and slept like, well, the dead. I would trot to our room and shake him as he lay tangled in his sheets, his mouth open and his face slack. He looked stupid, laying there like that. I never felt too bad thinking that, either, because he had much more in the looks department than me. We both had our father's dark shock of messy hair and slightly sunken eyes, and neither of us was going to claim more than our fifteen minutes based on our looks alone. But Mikey had gotten our mother's smile, according to Dad, and that made all the difference.

He had also gotten Dad's height, while I was a shrimp. Or *The Shrimp*—that's what Mikey called me, mostly with mild affection, sometimes…not so much. Once, when we were fighting, going at it over who knows what, he told me I would always be sickly looking because I'd come from Mum's cancer. We had both paused when he said that, him looking pale and shocked at himself, me filled with sudden, thick hatred. But that is what brothers do, right? What families do? We say things to hurt, and sometimes we're good at it. We know where to stick the knife, and how to twist it. Sometimes I think about that hurt, and how I still love Mikey, and Dad. That is what guilt is, I think. Hurt and love, all mixed up together.

I don't remember my mother, but there are a few photos of a gaunt, hollow-cheeked woman holding a tiny baby in thin arms, smiling bravely as her diseased body eats itself. Those pictures lived in an album in the back of the linen cupboard, deep in that cool mustiness that smelt like forgetting. I would pull them out sometimes, my heart thudding as I listened for the sound of my father arriving home, and I would look at myself in her arms, and try to remember the feel of her skin on mine. I never could.

There was another photo that hung on the wall, in which she is hale and whole, holding my chubby older brother. He stares at the camera, all serious and dark-eyed. And alive. I don't know where that photo is now.

Gone, like everything else.

Things changed the way they mostly do—sneaking up on you, disguised and smiling, but with one thick and eager fist curled and ready just out of your view. Dad was reading some stack of papers or maybe a report of some kind. I was picking olives off my pizza and piling them on the side of my plate while Mikey watched some crappy reality show. Whatever it was, the image suddenly froze.

"Hey!" Mikey said. "I was watching that!"

Dad put the remote down. "That stuff is crap."

Neither of us said anything. I don't know exactly what Mikey thought when Dad said things like that, but it twisted something inside of me. A worn twisting that I was so used to I almost didn't notice it. Like I almost didn't notice how he looked at me sometimes, frowning, his mouth pursing slightly as if he had recalled something unpleasant—the way a once-beautiful young woman had been consumed from the inside by disease and child both, perhaps.

It made a small wall of hesitancy and reserve between us. I remember one morning, standing at the kitchen door in my pyjamas and feeling the coldness of the wooden floor bite into my feet, watching as smoke billowed from the toaster. I might have been all of nine years old. Dad saw the smoke, cursed, and dropped the jar of jam on the floor, where it smashed.

"Fuck!" he yelled, but it was more of a growl, really. A surge of anger that couldn't quite get past his cramping throat. He closed his eyes. His face grew pale and his hands clenched into tight fists. "*Fuck* this! Fuck it all!"

A nine-year-old might have had a few different responses to seeing their father do that. They might have burst out crying. They might have run to their daddy, flinging their arms around him and offering comfort. I did neither of those things. Instead, I eased backwards through the kitchen door and went to get dressed, stepping quietly where I knew the boards would not squeak.

Now, with some goofy-faced wannabe celebrity frozen on the television and two boys staring at him from the floor, my father sighed.

"I want to talk to you both about something."

He must have read something in our faces, because he smiled a little then. Mikey might have gotten our mother's smile, but I loved Dad's. It shrunk the wall between us, if only for a moment. "It's something good," he added.

"I've been offered a promotion at work," he said. His smile grew wider, and I found myself smiling in return. Not that I really got it, but I kind of did.

"Partner?" Mikey asked, and Dad nodded, now grinning rather than smiling. Mikey jumped up and pumped a fist in the air. "Yes!"

I stood up as well, but didn't jump. I wasn't sure what it meant.

"It comes with a hefty pay bump," Dad said, looking at me, and that I did get. I had a sudden idea there might be a PlayStation in my future, like that goon Gavin at school owned. He'd been given one of the pre-release ones, and it had been the last thing that kid needed—the first thing being a punch on the nose.

Dad's smile faded. "But boys, it will mean a lot more work for me. I'm going to be busy. Busier, that is. There will be more late days for me. Most days."

That I didn't like the sound of, but we were used to him being away. More time to kill was nothing really, not for a couple of kids with their whole lives stretching out before them. So I shrugged and grinned and when Mikey gave Dad a hug, I did too. A big one, because Dad didn't often do hugs. And then we went back to the floor, and television, and later, ice cream. It was a good night. The last good one.

2

Dad working so much and then doubling down with the promotion wasn't such a big deal. Mornings were still a mess of rush and ill-temper, and we had more afternoons to kill by ourselves, but it was only Cooing and there was only so much to do.

Our home was on one of the five-acre blocks that buffered town from the larger parcels of land, one of the useless spaces the farmers sneered at and the townies aspired to. The school bus would drop us at the front gate, and we would charge down the wide dirt road and around the stand of wattles, racing to see who would get the television. Pointless, really, given Mikey's long legs (or my short ones), and I would usually veer off towards the kitchen in search of food.

With sandwich or biscuits in hand, I would wander out the back to where our scraggly lawn morphed into wild tangles of grass and blackberries, scattered with twisted eucalypts. There was one that was really good for climbing, but I had long ago mapped the routes to the thin branches that wouldn't hold my weight, and I rarely bothered any more. Mostly I kind of poked around. I wasn't supposed to. To be more accurate, I wasn't supposed to do so alone. It was Dad's one hard and fast rule—we were to stick together when he wasn't home. That rule held for all of five minutes on the first day he left us to our own devices. We just had to make sure we were both inside by the time Dad got home. Easy.

It was only a few days after Dad's promotion, and I was down on my hands and knees next to our boundary fence. Mikey was inside, watching one of his stupid music shows. Boring. I was more concerned with the fat brown caterpillar that was struggling over a small rock for no discernible reason.

"You know not to go near that dam," a voice said from very close by.

I looked up, swallowing hard in sudden surprise. There was a painful click deep in my throat.

"Sorry," Mr Jenkins said, his small, round face bright with concern. He gave me a companionable frown as he leant on the fence, his white, wispy hair floating in the breeze.

"Your dad at work?" he asked.

I nodded. Mr Jenkins was okay—Dad said so. I don't know how old he was, but he had that small, wiry build that some men seemed to shrink into as they aged. Just a little old guy who mostly kept to himself. His house, what I could see of it behind him and his own clump of eucalypts, was a small, weather-beaten thing, with an attached carport that sagged under an impressive layer of dead leaves. Parked underneath this precarious shelter was his worn but loved campervan. He went away in it quite a bit. You never knew when he would be gone, or for how long.

"I won't go near the dam," I said, because Dad had always said it was dangerous, and because Mr Jenkins was an adult, right there, looking at me.

He made a little waving gesture—two fingers together, twirling almost like a "get on with it" signal. It was a thing he did. Rude, I suppose, but he was a funny bloke.

"I know you know," he said, "but look."

I looked to where he pointed. Down the slope and through the long grass and low bushes was the dam. It was a holdover from before the land had been sliced up into small, sellable portions, a deep and murky affair filled with weeds and surrounded by steep, muddy banks. Out near the middle, an old drum floated. It never moved, even when it was windy.

Except for now. It had drifted over to the far bank, where it was almost lost in the shadow of a partially collapsed overhang.

"Don't you try and get it," Mr Jenkins said, regarding me with his watery grey eyes. "Your Dad might. Probably thinks it's an eyesore. But you keep away."

"Dad says it probably used to be a float for an old water pump," I said, looking back at the drum. It would be hard to get, even now. The overhang looked precarious, and I had no idea how deep the water was. It could be an inch, but it could be much more. "To keep the pipe out of the mud."

"Farm dams aren't safe," Mr Jenkins said.

"I know," I replied. This conversation wasn't going anywhere. I looked away from the dam and back down at the ground, but my caterpillar was gone.

"Good, good," Mr Jenkins said, but he must have been over the conversation too, because by the time I looked back he was already trundling off towards his little house behind the trees.

The rock I threw fell short and disappeared in the greenish water with a deep *splonk*. Mikey laughed and threw his own, which bounced off the drum. The hollow clang was everything my sad splash was not.

"We could pull it out," Mikey said as he hunted around for another rock.

I shook my head, even as a little worry-worm slithered into my stomach. I should've known Mikey would want to get it. It was the same as when he sprinted down the driveway to the house—he didn't really want to watch television. He just had to be first. Be noticed. Do *The Thing*, whatever *The Thing* happened to be. I knew how this would play out. Mikey would drag the drum out, with or without me, and then say nothing. It might take a day or a week, but eventually Dad would notice. Maybe when he dragged the mower out and attempted to clean up the yard, or on one of the warmer evenings when he sat out the back with a beer and told us to give him "a moment". Dad would be mad about Mikey screwing around with the dam, but I knew how Mikey would play that, too. It was on the edge, he would say. I didn't even get in the water.

"Dad said it's not safe," I said, instead of any of that.

Mikey rolled his eyes. "Come on, Shrimp! I'll toss you out with a rope around your waist. Easy!"

He grabbed me and started to drag me towards the water. I knew he was joking, but I also hated it when he grabbed me. I was so damn small, and it made me feel so helpless.

"Fuck off!" I yelled, and tried to jerk away from him. He flushed and shot a quick glance at the rectangle of Mr Jenkins' roof behind the trees. It wasn't likely he would hear us, but the last thing we needed would be Jenkins coming to see what was happening. Or calling our father at work.

Mikey jerked on my arm, hard.

"Shut up!" he hissed. "I'm only messing around!"

I jerked back and his grip slipped. I fell backwards and hit the ground hard enough for the air to whoosh out of me. I gasped and hiccupped while Mikey looked down, first with consternation and then with his face hardening in expectation. He knew what was coming next.

"I'm telling Dad!" I cried as soon as I had enough breath back.

"Fine," he snapped. "Go on then, Shrimp!" He turned and stalked away—not towards the dam, but towards the trees, pushing through the long grass with fitful sweeps of his arms. I almost shouted something shitty after him, but I didn't. At least there was that.

3

He drowned.

There is not much to say about the next few hours. Not much, and so much.

Dad came in to find me sitting in front of the television.

"Where's Mikey?" he asked, surprised to find me usurping Mikey's domain, sure, but it was also more than that.

"It's late," he said. When I glanced at the window I was

shocked to see it was dark outside.

He was looking outside as well, and frowning with mild worry—maybe more than mild. He didn't say anything else, just got up and went outside. Fast.

Then there was silence that bled outwards and all around, a silence that had nothing to do with the yammering of the television. I wanted to stand up and follow my father, but I just…didn't. I sat there and felt that silence rise up all around me, until I was like a fly stuck in honey. At some point a beam of torchlight swept across the windows, jittery and fast. Eventually the silence went away, and there was yelling. Shouting. I tried to get up again, to go to Dad, to see Mikey and make sure he was okay, but I couldn't. There was no way to know what had happened, but I did anyway.

It was night, Mikey was Mikey, and the drum had been right there. And of course, he had been pissed at me.

I stared at the television, not hearing it, not seeing anything. There were noises from outside, the awful snotty bawling of a grown man who I had never heard cry, and it got closer and closer. I thought of Dad, his hands clenched in the kitchen, whisper-shouting "Fuck! fuck this," and his puckered mouth when he looked at me sometimes. Only at me, but not Mikey.

The sound came to just outside the door, but not any further. I think there was some small part of my father that didn't not want me to see what he had brought back to the house. Or maybe even then my father couldn't stand the thought of me.

And then I kind of went away for a while. Next I recall Mr Jenkins was there, and Miss Abinathy, who lived three driveways down and sometimes came around when we were supposed to be asleep and snuck out before dawn. Someone turned the television off, and there were red, strobing lights outside.

"Probably shock," Miss Abinathy said quietly, and then someone picked me up and put me to bed. I think it was Mr Jenkins. I should have been too heavy for the little old man with the wispy hair and veiny hands, but I think it was him. And I was, after all, a shrimp. One lone Shrimp.

4

There were questions asked—whispered questions, inappropriate questions, formal, legal-type questions. There was some talk of me and Mikey being alone and unsupervised, but that didn't go anywhere. At one point before the funeral two police officers came and had a long talk with Dad in the kitchen while I sat on the floor in the next room, staring at the blank television screen. I didn't want to turn it on. I didn't want to touch it.

Much like my father didn't want to touch me. He held me each time he saw me crying, and told me it was an accident—just a terrible accident. But his arms around me were rigid, and it seemed he would draw back a little quicker each time, a little sooner than I wanted. When he spoke, I was sure I saw his mouth pucker a little and his gaze flatten.

The funeral tried to pierce me with rusted hooks of pain. In the years since I have realised that the true horror of tragedy is that it is so commonplace, so close to the surface of things. If you look too closely beneath your feet, you see things moving—grief, guilt, loss—hungry things that slither. All of them waiting for the bottom to fall out of your life, to grab you and pull you down, and down, and down.

Not that I thought any of that as the priest droned on in the cool cavern of the church, and my father sat next to me, his hands like bricks, his eyes dark. I stared at the coffin and wondered if it was monstrous to be so numb. One of Mikey's teachers gave his eulogy. I guess my father was doing his best just to survive the day, and the only other relative we had was my mother's brother, who couldn't be here. He was a man who visited rarely, a man who wore a suit and travelled to other countries for work at inconvenient times—like when his nephew died. He was coming, but my father could not wait.

I was not a pallbearer. I watched people who existed on the edge of our lives carry my brother away and thought that I felt nothing.

The house wasn't near big enough for all the adults that came for the wake. The rooms bulged with black-clad, dour-faced people who murmured loudly and picked at the corpse of our family and the sandwiches Miss Abinathy had organised.

"All alone, every afternoon."

That was from Mrs Garibaldi. She lived near the football oval. We would see her from the bus most afternoons drowning her front lawn with her garden hose and watching the street with glittering eyes. She followed her hungry words with a low clicking of her tongue—like she was mildly disappointed that the tragedy wasn't more overt. Spicier. Juicier.

I ignored her. I knew the fake pity I would see in her face, and dreaded the thought of her speaking to me. Probing, searching for more. I sat on the couch and pulled at the tight collar of the stiff dress shirt I would never wear again, and looked at the sandwich on the paper plate on my lap. The numbness I had felt was fading. Maybe Mikey wouldn't have done it if we hadn't fought. I thought about saying that. I wanted to get it out, sick it up, like it was something barbed and caught in my throat.

"It doesn't make any sense," Mrs Garibaldi continued, naked want in her voice. "He was the older. And he could swim."

Something cracked open inside me. I put my plate down on the couch arm.

"They say he got tangled up."

I don't know who said that, and I didn't look. I'd already heard it, and more besides. Mrs Garibaldi would get her fill, but not from me. I stood above a darkness full of pain, and those voices, those faces, were lined up behind me, eager for me to fall. It had been my fault and everyone should know it. They knew it already—they must. They were waiting for me to admit it. I couldn't.

I stood up slowly, a twelve-year-old made of glass, and went to my room—my room, now. Just mine. I closed the door and lay down on my bed, facing away from Mikey's side of the room. I couldn't look at his bed, his desk, all the pieces of his life he left behind. The voices beyond the thin wall were muffled, a low chorus of hollow words drilling away at what was left of my life.

I fell asleep on the edge of the deep hole of guilt, listening to the drone of vultures picking at our tragedy. And with sleep, I fell.

5

I knew it was a dream, but I did not try to wake. I did not even think of it. Everything was dark, a pitch-black emptiness that smelt of earth and an unpleasantness that wormed its way into my mouth and down my throat like paste—and then the late afternoon sun was cutting a slant of golden light across the kitchen table in a way that was as familiar as the fall of hair in my eyes. The theme song from one of the older *Doctor Who* seasons rose from behind me, and when I turned, I saw myself. I was sitting on the floor far too close to the television, my face saying more about the fight I'd had with Mikey than any enjoyment I was getting from watching the time-travelling Tom Baker and his multicoloured scarf.

I turned away from myself and pushed through the back door. It banged shut behind me, as it had done a thousand times before, and I walked over the cold grass and across the imaginary line my father insisted was there when he mowed. Beyond, the golden heads of the long grass clung and scraped against my legs. I stepped onto the steep bank near to where the drum had drifted, and my feet squelched as they sank slightly into the wet mud. It felt cold and very real.

Mikey was in the water already, pulling at the drum, trying to get it closer to the edge of the dam. He had taken his shirt off and he had a long streak of mud down his side. He grunted and pulled at the drum, which rolled obtusely in the water, bobbing and shifting and slipping away. His face was a red mask of frustration, and as I stood there he looked up, right at me.

"Fucking heavy thing," he said.

"Leave it," I said. "It's not safe."

He had not been speaking to me. He was not hearing or seeing me. He looked back at the drum.

"Fucking heavy," he said again, and then cocked his head.

"Dad says you're anchored. Maybe you're still caught up."

It *was* anchored. That had been whispered at the wake, and

before that, in my father's broken recounting to the police. There were lines under the water, slimy ropes that were old but still strong. After so long they had loosened enough to allow the drum to drift, but then had become tangled again. Twisting, grasping things, waiting below the muddy water. It did not matter that Mikey could swim. He had gotten his leg twisted in a duo of old, knotted anchor lines.

"Don't!" I screamed as Mikey took a quick breath and ducked under. That scream reverberated through the darkness that had opened inside me. Mikey did not hear it, but I hear it still.

The surface of the dam bubbled and then smoothed, and right as I was about to scream again, Mikey burst upwards. His eyes were wide and wild, and he lunged towards the overhanging bank. He thrust both hands deep into the mud, the soft, treacherous mud, and tried to haul himself forward. He managed to get out of the water almost to his waist, with the drum being pulled sluggishly behind him. And then his hands slipped out of the dirty brown clay and he slid backwards. The drum bobbed and rolled and shifted out a little in the water, and Mikey gave a cry and slipped back under. That cry—God, that cry.

I lunged forward—or tried to. I did not move. It was not like I was fighting against a wall or barrier or anything like that. It was more like when my father had run from the house in search of Mikey and I had just sat there, wanting desperately to go but knowing it would do nothing but hurt. I didn't move. I stared at the water, wanting to move, to plunge into the dam, to go for help. Instead, I screamed again. Even in the dream I felt something hard and sharp shift in my throat, a shard of panic and horror sharp enough to cut the innocence from my voice forever.

He probably could have still saved himself—pulled himself onto the drum, held it and tried to calm down, tried to disentangle himself. Maybe held on until his stupid little brother or his father came looking. Mikey surged upwards once more—or I guess that is what he tried to do. This time he misjudged the space above, or he was too panicked, and there was only a churn of water followed by a hard thump. I knew what that sound was, too, thanks to the black-clad whisperers in our home. Mikey had cracked his head on the drum.

I didn't scream again, but I moaned, long and low like an exhausted animal in a trap. I stared at the drum, at the settling water. Nothing else happened. Mikey was gone.

6

If I had woken as riled up as a grieving twelve-year-old could be, needing consoling, needing something my father could have easily offered, I don't think it would have stopped what was happening to me, but it might have stopped some of what came later. Maybe it could have knocked down the wall my father was so quickly building—or at least put me on the inside of it.

Instead, I woke sobbing, hard but quiet, my face wet and my nose running. The room was the grey of pre-dawn, and the house was still. The dream that felt like so much more was still with me, clinging to me like a thin film I could not breathe through properly. I rolled over and saw, through my tears, the pale outline of my brother's messy bed, the basketball balanced on his bedside table, even one school shoe upside down on the floor. All of it poised for his return—like he had slipped out into the colourless world that sat between the night and dawn, but not forever. His life was right there, across the room, waiting for him to come back.

I stared at Mikey's side of the room for a long time, trying to push the dream from my mind. It would not go. It had been so real. The whisper of the grass against my legs, the cold mud between my toes. The sound of my brother crying out. The grey light began to turn orange and pink as it bled over Mikey's bed, another day creeping towards me. Before it could touch me, I slid out of bed and slipped out of the room.

The house was a mess, but in a quiet, subdued way. There were a few platters of stale sandwiches on the table, their edges curled up in reproach at such neglect. I saw four of the good cups sitting on various surfaces, one still brim-full of black tea. There were two bulging garbage bags by the kitchen door, the door I had banged through in my dream only moments ago. I pushed it open tentatively and stepped outside, the wet grass cool beneath my feet, just as in my dream. This time I paused to slip on my old sneakers before I walked across the lawn and through the longer tangle of weeds. To my left I glimpsed Mr Jenkin's rooftop and his empty carport. Gone again already, even though he had been at the funeral and the wake. I might go too, if I could.

I reached the dam as the sun rose above the trees, turning the water a deep, bleeding red. In that baleful light I could see what I had come to see—the detail that had stuck like a fishhook in my mind.

The drum was unmoored well and truly now, and had drifted far out into the deeper water. I spared it no more than a glance. I was more interested in what I could see of the steep, almost overhanging bank next to where the drum had been in my dream. The morning sun hit the bared mud of that spot full on, and I saw the deep gouges that Mikey's hands had made as he surged forward and grabbed at land—grabbed at life. Exactly as I had dreamed.

I returned to the kitchen and let the door bang shut behind me in the way that usually elicited a rebuke, or at least a muttering, from Dad. He sat at the kitchen table, bleary-eyed and pale, and for a moment I thought I might be in for it—if he had known where I had been, or even that I had been out of the house unsupervised, given what had happened. But he did not flinch or even look at me. He just went on staring at the table.

I walked over and tried to put my arms around him. He stiffened ever so slightly, and then very carefully placed one arm around my shoulders, but his back had gone rigid and he kept himself slightly apart. I tried for a moment more, feeling awkward and blunted in some way, like an axe that had been struck on stone over and over. Then I dropped my arms.

He stood and went to the fridge. I sat at the table and stared out the window while I very carefully did not think about dreams or muddy finger gouges or the deep dark hole inside me.

He put a bowl of cereal with too much milk in it in front of me. I looked up, and for a moment I almost told him about the dream. But when I saw his sunken eyes and his pale face, his puckered mouth and the way his gaze shifted away from mine, I spooned up some cereal and shoved it in my mouth instead. He had always looked at me with blame for the death of my mother, but it had been blunted by time and love. Now I saw blame fresh in his eyes, and not much else.

"When you have finished you can help me clean," Dad said, and then walked out. There came the clink of cups being picked up, and after another tasteless spoonful of cereal, I got up and went to help.

There is nothing as meaningless as time after loss. Hours—or maybe it was a crawling lifetime—later, we ate a silent meal of leftover cheese sandwiches on curling, dry bread, washed down with half a cup of milk. I said good night to my father and went to our—my—room with an ache in my chest. Would I dream of my brother again? Would I watch him struggle, grasping at mud that bled through his fingers in his final moments? I stayed awake deep into the night, trying not to look at the grey shapes of his life across the room. I thought of myself, watching television as my brother gouged his hands into the muddy bank of the dam. I thought of my father's face as he realised something must be wrong, as he turned to run outside. Of my own inability to move, to follow, to acknowledge the hard knife coming down across the early evening, cutting our lives into before and after. And then I thought of Mrs Garibaldi and her hungry, wanting voice—*all alone, every afternoon*. It took a long, long time for sleep to take me.

7

I floated in a darkness that held me, compressed me. I was helpless. I was nothing but guilt and shame.

Come on, Shrimp.

All alone.

I closed my eyes and opened them again, but the blackness was absolute. There was the faintest smell of earth, and something bitter and unpleasant—rank, like the faded aroma of piss or rot.

"Hello?" I asked the dark, and then shut my mouth. I thought of those gouges in the mud. That had to be a coincidence, a shitty manifestation of grief and horror. Maybe I hadn't seen those gouges as they were at all, maybe that was only my mind retrofitting my dream to the real world. But then I thought of Mikey, looking up, looking through me, saying the drum was heavy but not speaking to me. Now I dreaded a voice. Let me be asleep. Let this be nothing.

The silence stretched out, and the blackness was unrelenting. I wanted to move, to sit up, to roll, but I couldn't. It was not quite like before. I felt confined, trapped, unable to move. When I had been there in the dark for what seemed a long time, there came a sound—a small, wet noise, close by my ear.

"Is…is someone there?" I whispered. The noise continued, and something moved, rustling and brushing against me.

I screamed and tried to jerk away, and the darkness pressed in against my face. I drew in a hot, heavy breath, and the rankness in the air intensified, coating the inside of my mouth like wax.

I waited for whatever had touched me to do so again. Nothing happened. Instead, I breathed the hot and heavy air. I tried again and again to move and could not. I lay in the dark for a long time.

I woke to the sound of whimpering, and that sensation of compression continued unabated. The familiar crack in my ceiling was backwards and upside down, a known thing that was odd and canted. I was laying on the floor, making the small, desperate noises myself. I must have twisted and turned violently as I slept, as I was wrapped from the chest down in my bedsheet like a soured candy in a wrapper, my pinned arms tingling. For a moment I still smelt something unpleasant, but then it resolved into the aroma of dried sweat and my own relief.

I had managed to untangle myself and was standing, shaking my arms and clenching and unclenching my fists when my father opened the door without knocking. He frowned and opened his mouth to speak, but then I saw his gaze shift across to Mikey's mess. His mouth did that weak puckering thing, and then his features smoothed out and he looked kind of up and past me, somewhere near my head.

"Time to get up," he said.

"What?" I asked blearily. I was tired, as if my journey through the darkness of sleep had done nothing but drain me.

He nodded once. "I've got work. You've got school."

<h1 style="text-align:center">8</h1>

I knew nothing of the expectations of grieving or of the adult world. I got dressed and sat in the kitchen with my cereal as my father prepared for his day. He did not speak beyond what was necessary, and I did not seek more. It was mostly silence between us until we reached school. My mind was full of that compressing darkness, the small noise near my head, the smell. But I was also thinking of that look from my father—that slight puckering as if I were a bad taste, and then that blankness, like I had the power to wipe thought from his mind just by *being*. When the car stopped, I put my hand on the door handle.

"Here," he said, holding out a ten dollar note. "Lunch."

I took it as my father spoke again.

"If anyone asks why you are back so early…"

I did not look at his face. Maybe I didn't want him to finish his thought. Maybe I was worried how he might be looking at me. With anger. With blame. Or with that new blank face, the one with everything smoothed away, a bare surface that had nothing left in it for me. The silence stretched on until I couldn't stand it.

"You've got work," I said. I sensed him shift slightly. I jerked on the door handle, scrambling clumsily out with my bag banging against my legs. I flung the door closed and started away, almost stumbling over the cracked concrete of the footpath. I didn't look back, not even when I heard the car start to move. My face burned and tears stung my eyes. I stopped, blinking furiously.

"Caleb? Cally? What are you doing here?"

It was Mr Cookson, the maths teacher, regarding me with his usual droopy gaze as he climbed from his battered station wagon. He ran one hand through his salt-and-pepper hair and then loosened his tie, even though he hadn't even made it into the building. I stared at him, uncomprehending. His was a world of rules—rigid school rules and the even stricter ones of algebra and operations set down on the page. A world of expectations and order. He had no place in my life now. He was like the early morning sunshine—pale, flimsy, fake. There was no pressing darkness here. No rankness in the warm, close air. And no Mikey grasping at a muddy bank.

"You should be at home," he said, stepping closer. For a moment I thought he was going to put a hand on my shoulder, but then he dropped his arm back to his side. He frowned at me instead.

I didn't say my father had work. I didn't say anything. I shook my head and squeezed my eyes shut, willing the stupid tears away. After a moment, Mr Cookson sighed. When I opened my eyes, he was not looking at me. He was staring over my shoulder at the school.

"Come on, then. Better here, I suppose."

I followed him in. It was okay until we went through the doors, and then it was not. This close to class time the halls were busy. I knew everyone—this was Cooing, after all—and I had a few friends, a few annoyances, and all the usual. Tommy, who was almost a head shorter than everyone else in class except me, and who I mostly got around with at recess and lunch—he might have come up to me, might have said something. But I didn't see him, and as I walked along the usual swell of chatter died. Not completely—it would take a lot more than sudden death to really silence so many pre-adolescents and teens, but it was like the lull between crashing waves. I became the ebb in the flow as I walked, and I did not look around. I was suddenly afraid. I was afraid I would see that blank nothing from my father's face reflected at me a hundred times over. They would know of my guilt. They must. I turned my mind away from the murmuring, away from the talk, what must have been talk of my fault, my lack. I turned away from that and back to thoughts of the darkness.

I sat at my desk, ignoring everything around me. Soon enough I was back in the dark, smelling piss and earth and something else unpleasant, a mix of things that might really be only the smell of one thing—terror. It was all so horrible and confusing, but it was also better. Better than thinking of Mikey grabbing at the soft, treacherous mud, or his cry as he slipped under the water. Better than thinking of my father's face as he looked at me with his features wiped clean of emotion.

I made it to recess. I might have made it the whole day, pretending I wasn't thinking about my brother dying and my father's face when he came home and asked where Mikey was—except for Gavin.

"Cally Cally Sally, you killed him, didn't you?"

I was sitting under the old pepper tree—far enough away from everyone to be alone, hopefully not far enough to instigate a drop-in from a concerned adult.

Cally Cally Sally.

It was better than Shrimp. Mikey had never let that one rip when we were at school. He was also the reason I usually only copped the occasional shove, the whispered *Sally*, a hard stare sometimes, but was mostly left alone. He had been a good big brother. The thought hurt, and that deep hole inside me widened a little more. I made a sound, something between a sigh and a low gasp.

Maybe Gavin wasn't as large as I remember. Maybe his hair was not so thin, his skin not so pale. What I do remember are the small crinkles he already had at the corners of his eyes, the smile marks of someone who found a lot of joy in his days. Someone who made his own joy, or took that joy from others with his large, soft hands and even softer words.

He stood there, smiling slightly as his lackeys fidgeted behind him. The strange orbit Mikey's death had put me in had already drawn pity from most, but looking at Gavin, I knew it had done nothing but piss him off. Different was different, regardless of why. I would need to be dealt with, and now it would be easy. It was just me.

All alone.

Cally Cally Sally. The Shrimp. The murderer.

I stared at him dully. He was big, and he was cruel, and he was right in front of me. I wondered why I had ever been afraid of him. Why I had cared. He belonged to that other world—a world of rules and expectations. It did not matter that his rules were not those of the adults or of the other children. He was part of a world that still had grounding, a world in which I had not killed and been consumed by grief and guilt.

I don't know what he saw in my gaze, or didn't see, but his face clouded over and his little crinkles lessened. I ignored that and shifted my gaze to his underlings, two boys that often floated after Gavin like pale, uncertain shadows. One of them rubbed their arms.

"Gav, let's leave him, eh? His brother just died."

As if that was a sudden realisation and not the reason for the visit. Gavin ignored him, as did I.

"You killed him, yeah? Little Sally, that's what I heard. You and him there all alone. What'd you do? Push him in? Hit him? I heard his head was cracked."

All alone, every afternoon.

Mrs Garibaldi's pitying voice was clear in my mind, but it was my father's face I saw. His face as he asked where Mikey was. His face twisted up as he regarded Mikey's side of the room, and the nothing that smoothed away all emotion as he shifted his gaze to me. My guilt ate at me, burrowed through me, leaving me hollow.

All alone.

There came a sudden stir of anger mixed with my guilt. It was not Gavin I was angry at, but he would do.

"Fuck you, Gavin," I said.

His soft, thick lips turned down in a frown and his eyes narrowed. A pink flush began to creep up his cheeks and he bawled his fists as he opened his mouth again. I knew where this was going. I was Cally Cally Sally, I was the Shrimp, and I was all alone. My anger turned into something heavier and more solid. Fuck Gavin. Fuck Mikey. And fuck my father.

Gavin took half a step forward and then a full step back as I launched myself at him, screaming. He reared, pulling his head up and away as I swung at him, my small fist knotted into a tight ball that held all my pain and confusion at what had happened, at what was still happening. I took Mikey's death and the silence in the house and my warped dreams and I flung it all straight at the bully's face. There was a crack and a sharp pain as I connected, mashing his top lip and driving one tooth through the thin skin of my knuckle. The sensation cut through my anger and confusion like nothing else had, and I had a moment of utter certainty that something profound had happened—profound and horrible— that the opening of that dark space inside me, that repository of loss and self-hatred, had somehow caused the dark dreams. That my guilt had first hollowed me out and then cracked me open in some strange fashion, and I was now bound to some horror I knew nothing of.

Gavin cried out and lifted one hand to his mouth. His lip was badly split and blood dribbled down his wrist. He wiped at it and then stared at his hand.

"You shit!" he shouted, and I saw one of his front teeth was chipped. Good. My hand throbbed, and I shook it. A few drops of blood flew off and some of it spattered against the face of one of the other boys. He backed away a few steps, his hands raised as if to ward me off. Dimly, I heard an adult yelling, but that didn't matter. That was in another world.

I laughed. It came out in a great looping peel. Gavin blanched at the sound, but then bunched his fists and swung at me. I tried to duck but I was laughing, laughing at the ache inside me, at the thought of being all alone, every afternoon, of Mikey grabbing me in nasty jest, pulling me towards the dam, of me saying I was telling. Gavin's meaty club of a hand smacked a glancing blow off the side of my head, high up, and I felt nothing. I punched him again, an ineffectual looping blow that hit him in the neck. And then he was close, too close, and he pushed me down. The ground was hard and I grunted as I hit it, my face grinding against the dirt. His foot sunk into my stomach and all the air rushed out of me in a sharp *woof*. The yelling was suddenly close, right there, and someone grabbed Gavin just as I seized his leg. He tried to jerk away but I clamped on. He was in my world, now. There were no rules here. I twisted my head and sunk my teeth into his calf, and when he screamed, I bit down harder, trying for blood. Then someone was pulling at Gavin, and someone else put their hands on me. Adult hands, large and grasping, and suddenly I was somewhere else.

It was only for a moment. I was in the dark again. There were shadows on shadows, and that unpleasant smell returned. The small, wet noise came again, somewhere nearby, but it was softer, fading. Weaker.

And then it was all gone and I was being hauled up off the ground. I looked up to see Mr Cookson, he of the droopy eyes and loose tie, holding on to me as another teacher held Gavin by one arm and tried to inspect his leg.

9

Mr Cookson sat beside me outside the principal's office. He did not ask me about the fight. For a while he did not say anything at all, but as the minutes lengthened, he started to shift minutely. I think he was unsettled by my ongoing lack of...*anything*. I suppose he thought I was caught up in what had happened—the fight, or my grief, or both. And I was, but mostly I was thinking about that moment of darkness. It was like when I was asleep, with the darkness pressing in on me, the air full of the smell of earth and something like rot. But this time I had not been asleep. What Gavin had said to me, and the anger and confusion I had experienced, had made me feel the same, though—the same as when I had lain in bed while the wake went on beyond the thin wall, and the same as when I had first dreamed of that cloying dark. I had fallen into the deep hole of guilt inside myself. I had laughed as it happened this time, swinging my Shrimp fist at Gavin as I did, seeking a release. But that had not been enough. That emptiness inside me was more than emptiness—dark called to dark, in some twisted way. I had been filled with something else, and I was drinking the horror of it, sleep or no.

Mr Cookson cleared his throat.

"If... If you need someone to talk to, Caleb," he began, and then stopped.

I could tell him, I realised. Tell him of the darkness, the guilt, how it had grown inside me until it had become too much. That my horror at what I had done had hollowed me out and cracked me open and connected me to something worse. That this had happened because it was what I deserved. I could tell him all that, but it would have to start with me telling him that I had killed Mikey.

I said nothing, and then the moment was past. There was movement outside the office window, and I looked up to see my father, wearing his blank face.

More silence then, in the car, with my father staring at the road as we made our way back to the house that should have felt like home. Silence as I sat and tasted the ghost of Gavin's blood in my mouth and my now bandaged hand throbbed and my stomach ached from the bigger boy's boot. And still silence as we walked inside, me letting the kitchen door swing shut with a bang that should have roused my father but did not. It was barely lunchtime. My father looked around the room, his face pared back to nothing.

"I'm going to have to go back to work," he said without looking at me.

"Dad," I said. My stomach ached from more than the booting. I was angry, but I couldn't give voice to that. I was more than angry, though. "Dad, I'm sorry."

He did not move for a long time. Finally he turned towards me, and I saw the featureless plain of his face almost crack. His mouth puckered and then flattened, and he blinked twice, quickly.

"I have to go," he said. His voice trembled at these first words, and then dropped into flatness. "Don't go outside."

He turned to the door and I felt something bubbling up inside me—more than guilt and grief and confusion. It was like what I had felt with Gavin, but more—an aching, burning hurt, an anger fuelled by the unfairness of it all, fuelled by my father's sudden refusal to at least *try*. I would even take the clenched fists, the low growling *fuck, fuck it all*. Or even a *fuck you*. Something. Anything.

I ran to the door and banged through it, already several steps behind him as he walked—no, hurried—to the car.

"You're going?" I cried in a high, glassy voice. I could feel heat rising up my neck, spreading across my face.

He did not turn around. "I have to get to work."

"Dad!" I yelled, as snot touched my upper lip. My vision blurred as he reached the car. "Dad! I'm sorry!"

He paused then, the car door half open, and a silence fell between us. I could hear myself snivelling, trying not to sob, and I could hear my father breathing much more heavily than he should have. A callous magpie called in one of the eucalypts, and a light breeze moved the tall grass beyond the mown edge. I thought for a moment that he would close the door and turn back to me, hug me, say something. Tell me I was horrible or tell me everything would be okay. Tell me it was all my fault or that it wasn't. I drew in a huge, wobbling breath, and tried for hope rather than dread.

And then the moment passed, and my father pulled the door all the way open.

"Stay inside," he said without looking at me. His voice wavered again. I stood there as he reversed along the driveway. His eyes were on the rearview mirror, not on me. He was crying as well, I think, but everything was still blurry enough that I could not be sure. I hoped that he was. It would be better than that *nothing* look.

The funeral, the dreams, school and Gavin, and then my father leaving as I cried, broken and begging—it was too much. Standing there in the dusty driveway with the heat of the high sun suddenly beating down, I yawned widely through my tears and then winced as the gravel rash on the side of my face stung.

I turned back to the house, my gaze skipping past the dam and the floating drum as if they were points of star-bright fire that could burn my eyes.

Mr Jenkin's camper was in his tired old carport, and as I took a few steps towards the house I saw our neighbour himself standing by the fence. He was too far away for me to make anything out but I felt my face flush anew. He must have heard me yelling at my father, and maybe seen him leave — leave me here, a day after the funeral of my brother. I turned quickly and went inside.

The day fell on me as if it meant to finish grinding me flat. I blinked heavily and tried to think of something to do other than sleep. I dreaded the pressing darkness and the hot, rank air. I did not want to think of that small sound, that light brush against my face. My new world had no rules, and I was afraid the dark of my dreams might not be empty the next time I slept. I sat on the couch and turned on the television. I yawned again as some voice droned on, the bright colours becoming muted as I struggled to keep my eyes open. I was twelve, and I was tired, but I do not think it was sleep that took me. Like in the playground with Gavin, I was there, and then I was not.

10

I was in the dark again, but it was lighter, a muted thing of shadows and folds. It was like standing within the well of grief and guilt that was now the centre of me. I could see nothing of substance, and I was trapped.

The air held the same mild stench as before. I tried moving forward and felt my feet touch a solid surface which I could not see. The smell grew slightly more distinct as I moved—a wet mustiness, low and pervading, but almost overridden by a stronger scent, riper and rotten. I gagged a little and then tried to breathe shallowly through my open mouth. That made it feel like a living thing lay on my tongue, curling its fetid body up behind my teeth and crowding my throat. The smell and the shadows combined into something claustrophobic yet unreal, and I put my hands out in front of me, desperate to feel anything concrete. Outlines and vague shapes retreated before me. I thought of that wet sound next to my ear while I had lain in the dark, of something rustling and then brushing against me. My hands shook, but I kept them stretched out.

And then I brushed something hard and pointed and small with my palm. It gave slightly before I pulled my hand back. For a moment I saw nothing but shadows upon shadows, but as I bent forward and peered closely, the shape in front of me resolved into something.

I screamed and staggered back a few steps. The shape became indistinct once again, which was somehow worse. Tentatively, I moved forward again. There was a hand in front of me. Just a hand, the wrist disappearing into the indistinct darkness. It was palm up, curled into a partial claw, the fingers pointing upwards. The thing was pale and emaciated, to the point that I could see the bone of two knuckles where the papery skin had torn. What was left of the flesh was greyish white and sagged grotesquely from the fingers, as if the whole thing had started melting. The nail of the ring finger hung askew, broken and ragged. I had brushed what little was left of the index finger with my open palm.

I drew in a huge, whooping breath to scream again. Instead, I got a lungful of that thick, almost ripe air and I gagged and bent to throw up. Nothing came out.

I took another step back and my feet tangled together. I went down on my backside, hard, and caught the tip of my tongue between my teeth. There was pain, but I barely registered it. I sucked in another lungful of the fetid air, and screamed again. And then again.

11

"Caleb, Caleb! Wake up!"

The shout came with not-quite mild shaking. I was still screaming. I struck out with one hand partially closed, and felt it crack against something. The pain in my split knuckle flared, doing more to draw me into wakefulness than the shaking or shouting. There was a grunt and a muttered curse, and the fingers curled around my shoulders tightened painfully for a moment before disappearing.

I sat up, groggy and disorientated, blinking in bright, painful light. I tasted blood and felt the sharp pain where I had bitten my tongue. My father sat beside me, his expression one of either concern or impatience. One of his eyes was watering.

I rubbed at my face rather than continue looking at him. It must have been late, or at least not early, given he was home.

"I had a bad dream," I mumbled, even though I knew, *I knew*, it was more than that. Like watching Mikey drown. Like laying in the stinking dark with something brushing against me. Standing in the shadows seeing that dead hand was more than a dream. *Oh God, that hand!*

Dad went very still and didn't say anything. I rubbed my face again, and when I realised it was getting a bit stupid to keep doing so, I dropped my hands and looked at him. His face had gone back to that blank, nothing place. I thought of Mikey surging up from the water, crying out, and of the hand with the grey skin sloughing off it. There were horrors in my head, in my sleep and in the dark, which made the horrors in my waking world seem… not less, just something that could be grasped.

"I said I was sorry," I said. It was too big, too much for a kid to hold on to forever. I was sorry for Mikey. Sorry for not being with him, not realising what was happening, not saving him. And I think I was also saying I was sorry for being me, and not him. I knew Dad couldn't see me without seeing my mother in her final months, wasting away, drained of life and future, and now he couldn't see me without seeing the waterlogged corpse of Mikey, the son that had borne his wife's smile.

"I know you are," my father said without looking at me. His eye was still watering. Maybe both eyes.

"We…we had a fight," I said, my voice dropping to a whisper. I didn't want to say it. I wanted to tell him about the dreams. About the darkness, about that hole inside of me, and about what was happening. But I couldn't do that. I couldn't tell him I had seen Mikey drown or that I had seen him grasping desperately at the mud of the bank, his eyes wide as he cried out. I couldn't tell him about a rotted hand in the dark.

My father didn't say anything for what felt like a long time. I waited, my heart thudding heavily in my chest. I thought again of my dreams, the funeral and wake, even Gavin and my throbbing hand, the ache in my stomach from the bully's boot. And I saw again that pale, rotten hand, and I tasted my own blood in my mouth. All of that meant nothing as I waited for my father to speak.

"Where…" he begans and then stopped. He would not look at me. He made a sound like he was choking, like he had a fishbone stuck in his throat.

"Where were you? You were supposed to stay together."

It was like Gavin's kick to my stomach, and it drove the wind from me. I dared a look at him but only for a second. That second was an eternity too long. His face was not blank anymore—what must have been the thinnest veneer had cracked and splintered. He was crying, his face twisted, his sunken eyes already red. I don't know if there was real hatred there. In a way it would be easier if I knew that for sure. But I do think I saw failure, and the release of something that was too big, too messy for him to deal with. What he was saying was so unfair.

Even as I looked away from him, he doubled over, gasping and sobbing. It was like he had sicked, up not just words but some poison that had been festering inside, eating him up, and yet getting it out had not helped. It had only broken him open wider, flooded him with grief and guilt and shame. I knew what that felt like.

I drew in my own breath. A small part of me noted the cleanliness, the freshness of the air and the lack of rot, but mostly my mind was in turmoil. I had killed Mikey. I had not pushed him under, but I had left him when I'd promised not to. I had argued with him, and then I had sat and watched a re-run of a show I had seen before while he floundered and struggled and lost his life. I knew I was at fault. I had known it—why else would I have riven myself as I had, opening that dark space inside me that led me to these new visions, this new world where shadows pressed against you and the stench of death led you towards dead horrors—the way to such a place was through guilt.

But still…

All alone. Every afternoon.

"Where were *you*?" I bawled. I couldn't see him properly, because my tears were suddenly streaming again, but that was okay. I squeezed my eyes shut and said it again, the thing that had been tumbling over and over in my head, the thing that I had screwed up into my fist and thrust into Gavin's teeth.

"Where were you, Dad?"

I wish I could take it back. Saying it did nothing to ease my own aching grief or lift the heavy stone of responsibility, and it did nothing to pull me back from the dark world I had found myself in. All it did was tear my father open even wider.

He clenched his fists so tightly they went white, and I thought he was going to hit me. But then he cried out and bent over again, so far forward he almost pitched off the couch. His shoulders shook and he rocked back and forth, grunting.

As he rocked upright, I put a hand on his shoulder. It scared me to do it, scared me almost senseless, but I was horrified at what I had done with my words. He flinched away as if I had burnt him, and then rose and stumbled across the room. He disappeared down the hallway without looking back, and a moment later I heard his bedroom door click shut. I sat very still for a moment as the tears ran down my face, and then I stood and walked very slowly and carefully to my own room.

12

I dreaded what might come with sleep, and I feared it would come regardless. I lay on my bed and stared across the room at the pieces of Mikey's life as the tears dried on my face. I think I was waiting for my father to come in, to speak to me, maybe to try and present some fragments of family so we could begin to stitch it back together. He did not come and I could not bring myself to walk down the hall and tap on his door. I kept thinking of him in the kitchen, his hands balled into fists—*fuck this. Fuck it all.* Despite my earlier wish to hear something from him, even if only those words, I could not bear the thought of it now. As the moon finally rose and cast a dull light through the window, stretching my brother's things into silhouettes of pain and loss, I rose and pulled on my shoes.

I closed the ill-treated kitchen door softly. I doubted my father would hear, or rise if he did, but I wanted no more confrontation with him. I could not imagine what to say after the last, or how to break down that mammoth wall of silence he had built by closing his bedroom door.

At first, I had no idea of what I was doing. After what felt like a lifetime of exhaustion and confusion, I was very awake—not refreshed, but far from sleep. The night was still, and the almost full moon cast the world in greys and blended shadows that hinted at familiar surrounds but did not reveal them. I walked to the edge of the lawn and looked towards the dam, nothing but a blackness against the moonlight. I had no desire to go there, not now, not ever.

There was a light on at Mr Jenkin's house, just visible through the stark black outlines of the trees. I wanted someone to talk to. A twelve-year-old dealing with grief might want that, should want that, and I had more than just grief. I was so afraid, and not only of the horror of the visions themselves. I had the sense that whatever barrier was holding my waking and dreaming worlds apart was fraying, breaking down, a crumbling wall battered by the waves of my own guilt and confusion. What had happened with Gavin—that had not been a dream, I was sure. And later, on the couch, that had felt a lot more like falling behind a thin veil than falling into sleep itself. Something had happened to me, and even more frightening, it was still happening. I thought I might be going mad, if a twelve-year-old could really think such a thing.

I turned to the driveway and started walking, the crunching of my shoes on the gravel loud in the night. I do not know what time it was, but the road was an empty strip of darkness that I passed over very briefly. Mr Jenkins's mailbox was close to ours, and I turned down his own short driveway without hesitation. The way was clear in the pale moonlight.

A sensor light came on as I stepped onto the pavers at the front door, and there was barely a pause between my light knock and the door opening. Mr Jenkins stood there in pyjama bottoms and an old long-sleeved shirt. He wore thin slippers, and his ankles below his pants were thin.

"Caleb?" he asked, concern in his voice. "Is everything alright?"

That was enough to do it. I started blubbering, my shoulders heaving.

"No!" I cried. "No, nothing is!"

He was clearly uncomfortable. He brushed at his wispy hair and then patted me awkwardly on one shoulder as I cried in his doorway. After a brief hesitation he ushered me through to his own kitchen and dithered about making a cup of tea he must have known I would not drink. I sat at the table and tried to settle myself. It was surprisingly easy to stop crying, at least. I think I was close to being cried out. I was exhausted in mind and body.

Mr Jenkins placed the tea in front of me and sat down across the table. He looked at me with those watery eyes of his as he sipped his own tea. I glanced around the kitchen—I had never been inside his house before. It was smaller than ours but seemed about the same vintage. There was even a screen door next to the fridge that opened out to the dark back yard. Off to one side there was a closed door that in our house would open on to the hallway that led to the bedrooms. It was all very neat and had that mild old person smell that is so recognisable to all but the aged themselves.

"Can't sleep, I suppose?" he asked. "How are things with your dad?"

"Not…not good."

"Hmm. I see."

He fell silent, but that, in itself, was a comfort. He did not offer platitudes, and I thought that maybe he would not dismiss what I said. Dad had always said that Mr Jenkins was a good neighbour. That we could go to him if we needed. I knew he didn't mean about this, of course, but still…

"I keep having dreams," I whispered. "Bad dreams."

"Bad? Like what?"

"I…I see Mikey drowning."

Mr Jenkins took a long sip of his tea, his eyes not leaving my face.

"I'm not surprised, Caleb. It was a terrible thing, and it has only been a few days. I hate to say so, but you may have dreams like that for quite a while. It's normal."

"No," I said quickly. "No, I mean I really see him drowning. I see him trying to get out, going back under, hitting his head…"

My voice failed on that last, and even though I thought I was done crying, I felt wetness on my face once again.

He frowned. "That sounds horrible, Caleb, but it *was* horrible. Like I said, you might have those kinds of dreams."

"It's more than that!" Now that I had begun, I wanted to see it through. Explain it. Get it out and away from me, if I could. "I'm empty, and there is darkness…"

I wanted to say there was a hole inside of me. That I had killed Mikey by not being with him, by being a stupid little brother and fighting with him over nothing. I wanted to tell Jenkins that I ached, and when the guilt tore me open each time anew, the emptiness inside was filled with shadows and pressing darkness and a curled, dead hand. But I didn't think I could.

He didn't respond. He just looked at me, and after a bit I realised, he was giving me time to work my way through whatever it was I needed to say.

"It feels so real," I began, but that was not right. I took a deep breath.

"The first time—I mean the second time—after I dreamed of Mikey, everything was dark. I couldn't move, and there was a noise. A quiet, wet kind of noise. It smelt bad." I did not say something touched me. What I had said sounded weak enough, so much like a dream, anyway. I shook my head in frustration and then blurted out what I really didn't want to say.

"There was a hand! A dead hand with the skin hanging off it."

Mr Jenkins drew back a little. He opened his mouth but seemed to be at a loss. Finally, he looked down into his cup and then looked at mine.

"More tea?"

I shook my head, and he stood and walked past me. I twisted around to watch him. He started talking to me over his shoulder even as he rummaged in the cupboard.

"That sounds terrible, Caleb. I don't know what to say about what it might mean, but you must remember that you have been through something traumatic. You are going to be processing it in a lot of different ways." He fussed about for a moment more and then turned to come back.

"What does your father say about it?"

I shook my head.

"I haven't told him. I can't tell him. He…he thinks it's my fault." That hurt to say. It hurt to think, as well.

"Caleb, it is not your fault. You are a child. If anyone is at fault, it is your father."

I looked up at Mr Jenkins, shocked to hear an adult say such a thing. And he was wrong, I knew that. My father was to blame, yes, of course, but so was I. Mikey was dead. There was plenty of blame to go around.

He put his mug down on the table next to mine. It was empty, which was odd. I glanced at it and then back at him, and that was when he brought his now mug-less hand up and covered my mouth and nose. I tried to jerk away, and he stuck me in the neck with something sharp. Again, I tried to twist away, but like I said, he was strong—stronger than you would think. I gasped in surprise and tasted old man sweat and dirt. I tried to grab him but all I did was knock his mug onto the floor where it smashed. The sound of it seemed far away, and then the room was moving sideways, and I felt Mr Jenkins's hand on the back of my head, lowering me gently down.

13

I sat up, woozy and unable to focus. No—I was already sitting up, leaning against a wall. My mouth was full of an odd, metallic taste, and it was all I could smell as well. My stomach churned and clenched. I closed my eyes as I dry-heaved and then sat back, raising a hand to wipe spit from my mouth. Or I tried to. I couldn't lift my arm, and when I opened my eyes and looked, I saw my wrists were bound with thin blue twine. I closed my eyes again and leant back. A cold, damp surface pressed against the back of my head.

"Sorry, Caleb," a voice said. "That's the tranquiliser."

I opened my eyes yet again and tried to focus. At first my head swam and nothing would hold steady, but after a moment things settled. The room was dark, but at the top of a flight of rough concrete stairs there was a slightly ajar door that let in a small spill of light. Jenkins stood in the middle of the room, still in his long-sleeved shirt, pyjama bottoms and thin slippers. He held a shovel. I could not see beyond him—there was nothing but shadows where the light from the door did not reach.

"What… What is going on?" I croaked. I tried to get my feet under me but had no success, and I saw then that my feet were tied together with twine as well.

"I might ask you the same thing, young man," Jenkins said in a disapproving tone. "At first I thought you must have been spying on me, even though I am ever so careful."

He shook his head. "But of course not. You are sensible enough that it would have been the police visiting me, not yourself. I can only guess you actually did somehow stumble across my activities as you have said." He chuckled. "Who would have thought? Incredible, in its way. But it can't be allowed."

He cocked his head to one side and gave me that companionable little frown of his, as if inviting me to appreciate something. "I was going to put you in the wall. I thought you might be a good addition." He held up the shovel as if to underline his point.

"But I have realised that just wouldn't do. It has been quite uncomfortable already, with so many people around after your poor brother's death. Even police," he said, stepping forward, his eyes wide. "Can you imagine?"

He shuddered as if at a particularly unpleasant thought, and then bent down to something on the floor.

"Wall? What? Mr Jenkins… What?"

I still felt woozy, and I breathed out hard, trying to get that sweetness out of my mouth and nose. I hoped some clarity might come with the fresh air, but when I breathed in, I almost heaved again. The air was full of that ripe, rotten stench that had been much fainter in my dreams. Now it was mixed with a wet, mouldy mustiness. Jenkins looked up at my distress.

"Yes, sorry about that. An unfortunate side effect." He paused, standing up and breathing deeply. "But, you know," he continued, "you do get used to it. And it makes me think of all my efforts over the years. Of my lovely wall." With that he pointed—at me, I thought at first, but then I realised he was pointing beyond me. To the wall. I tilted my head back and around as much as I could.

I didn't scream, so I guess my previous time in the dark had been good for something, but the air left me in a kind of quick sigh. Above me and to the left was the hand from the darkness. I knew it. I recognised the sagging skin, the exposed bone of the index finger, and how the fingers all curled upwards as if trying to hold on to the last vestiges of life. Instead of darkness and shadows at the wrist, the hand disappeared inside the wall, which was made of hard-packed earth.

I was going to put you in the wall.

My gaze moved on past the hand. I couldn't help myself. Maybe it was my own morbid fascination, the lure of horror suspended in disbelief. It doesn't really matter. I saw what I saw.

It was another hand, this one close to skeletal. The digits were held together by the thinnest parchment of dried flesh. The ring finger was missing and glancing down I spied it on the dirt floor, a pale grey shape half bent in a come-hither gesture.

Further along the wall to the left there was another hand. And another beyond that, lower down, almost at knee height. I turned to the right and saw four more, spaced far apart. They stuck out haphazardly from the wall like weird, pale growths that had burst forth seeking light and space but found death instead. Two were dry, desiccated things. One was covered in grey, sagging skin, like the first I had seen. And one was…fresh. That one stuck out from a large hole in the wall, and there was a fresh pile of dirt on the floor below it.

I thought you might be a good addition.

"What—what is this, Mr Jenkins?" I asked, in the trembling voice of a child who knows the answer, dreads the answer, but still hopes there is some unknown facet of adult life that can explain away what they are seeing.

He was watching me closely, his eyes very bright in the dim light.

"It's my wall," he said softly. "My wall. You know, I am very sorry about this, but in a way I am glad. I have always wanted someone to see this. I mean, others have, but they haven't really been in an…let's say *appreciative* state."

He waved a hand. "It has taken me a long time. Got to be careful, you know."

He came forward, a little man with wispy hair and his thin ankles sticking out of his pyjama pants, his slippers crunching on the gritty floor. I flinched a little to one side as he got close, but I could not go far with my legs tied together. He gave a small, distracted smile at that, and then reached out and very lightly touched the protruding bone fingertip of the hand I had dreamed of.

"This one, he came from Sydney. Six hours' drive to get there, of course, plus so much longer looking. So many things have to converge, but eventually, they always do. It was very late, and he was very drunk. I think he was walking home."

As he spoke, he reached out again and trailed his fingers across the stiff digits of the hand. Then he stepped to another, touching it carefully. Tenderly, even.

"The trick is to have no pattern. Over thirty thousand people go missing in Australia each year. That's about one every eighteen minutes. But even with that, you have to be patient, of course. The wall helps with that. I come down here and look at it, and feel at peace. For a while."

He turned to look at me again, his finger tapping the dead hand in front of him.

"This one… Homeless, I think, but she said she was only hitch-hiking." He lowered his voice a little. "Some people, you just can't trust what they say." He paused, as if lamenting the state of things, and then shook his head. "Ten hours' drive from here, on the side of the road. Quite a nice little surprise, she was, standing there, waiting. I didn't have to wait, didn't have to spend time looking around. Sometimes it's like that," he concluded, matter-of-factly.

"I…I won't tell anyone." Clichéd, sure, but what else was going to come to mind for a kid? Or anyone, in such a situation?

He ignored that. He stepped across to the hole in the wall, the one with the relatively fresh hand sticking out of it. I was glad I couldn't see into the space itself.

"Funny, this one. He was about my age. I almost didn't take him. Only two hours away, but in the end, it was only me and him at the campground. And I had been good for quite a while." Jenkins turned to look at me. "You don't shit where you eat, you see. Two hours is very close."

He made a face. "Sorry about the language," he added, and then began to stroke the stiff hand. "My guest here has finally passed, and this should already be filled in, but Mikey caused quite a bit of inconvenience for me. What with first seeing what the fuss was about, and then the funeral. There were lots of people around." He looked down at me. "Sorry," he said. "I don't mean to be insensitive."

Watching him touch that dead hand so tenderly as he apologised and worried about offending me… I think that was what did it. I could not have ever dreamed this or made it up. I was horrified, of course, but deep in that darkness that now lived inside of me, I was not surprised. This was a new world. One without rules, one in which guilt and grief ate you from the inside out and were preludes to horrible things. I looked at the fresh hand our mild little neighbour was stroking softly, and I thought of that cloying darkness I had dreamed of after Mikey. Of the small, wet noises, and the feel of something brushing against me. I wondered if in that hole, in that darkness, there was someone who had struggled to the end. Someone who had been tied up, maybe gagged, only able to move slightly, to make tiny pleading sounds that no one could ever possibly hear. *Yes*, I thought. And had it already been too late when I had dreamed of that? I thought also *yes*, just like the dream of Mikey's death. This was a curse, after all. Not a gift.

"I want to go home," I said as I started to cry. Again.

Mr Jenkins shook his head slightly, even as he kept touching the dead hand.

"I am sorry, Caleb. And your poor father—I suspect this will break him, well and truly. It is a shame. You are good neighbours. You leave me alone."

He made a rueful face, a little hard to see in profile. "Well, mostly."

He finally stopped touching the hand and turned to me. "No point putting it off. I was going to put you in the wall, but that would cause all sorts of issues, I imagine. Unfortunate intrusions, searches, maybe. So I think you might have to drown in the dam, like Mikey. Maybe racked by guilt? Overwhelmed? You are a bit young for such depths of despair, but I don't think anyone will really questions it. Hmm?"

I shook my head, trying to negate it all even as I began sobbing harder. Every time I drew breath I tasted that stench, the smell of rotting people. I could only imagine how much worse it would have been if they weren't all mostly buried. Jenkins was… I could not understand it. He was a monster, and yet he was somehow still our pleasant old neighbour. I wonder, now, if that was how he managed it for all that time. He was not wearing a mask, not hiding, really. He was just showing part of his true but fractured self.

He made a *tsk*ing sound. "I have to pop up and grab some more twine. Can't have you wriggling your way free while I carry you. But there is no sense you getting all worked up in the meanwhile."

He walked back over to where he had been standing when I woke. He bent down again and quickly finished unrolling a large piece of canvas. While he did that, I tried to jerk my legs free, but all I got for the trouble was a sharp pain where the twine bit into the thin flesh of my shins. I shook my head to try and clear my vision and then made a desperate lurching kind of lunge towards the stairs. All that happened was I flopped sideways to lay on the ground, even more uncomfortable than I had just been.

"Now, now," Jenkins said. "That's what I mean. Let's have none of that. I'm not as young as I was when I started this. I can't really manhandle people like I used to." He smiled cheerfully as he approached, looming over me as I strained to look at him from my awkward position. He held up a small brown bottle and a syringe filled with liquid. "I don't want to break a hip, or anything."

He bent down and stuck me in the neck again. It didn't hurt as much as the first time, but that was probably the grogginess

I was still dealing with. It came on as quick as before, and I watched from a darkening tunnel as Mr Jenkins stood up with a satisfied look on his face.

14

I dreamed. Of course I did, because being forced to see Jenkins and his earthen-walled horror room didn't excuse me from my own guilt. Even being bound and wrapped in canvas and dumped in the same dam my brother had drowned in was not enough.

I was in our kitchen. The pale moon turned everything into outlines and washed-out shapes. The lawn through the window was an aged, colourless polaroid of grass backed by the bright, cold pinpricks of stars. Through the black and crooked lines of tree branches, I could see a light on at Mr Jenkins's. He was up. He was busy.

A door banged open behind me, and I turned, startled, as my father rushed into the kitchen. He wore a pair of old tracksuit pants and nothing else. His thin chest was very pale in the light of the moon, and his eyes were wide and dark. He was panting as if he had run a race rather than having just emerged from his bedroom. I felt my throat constrict at the sight of him.

He did not look at me and I did not bother saying anything, even though I wanted to say so much. It had not worked with Mikey and it would not work now. He sprinted past me and hit the screen door hard, sending it flying back to smack against the wall with a ferocity that made all of my previous efforts pale in comparison. I ran after him. He should have easily outstripped me, but in the way of sleep and dreams, and perhaps in the way of cursed visions, I kept pace well enough.

He had no shoes on, but it did not slow him as he ran across the lawn and into the longer grass. I knew from experience there were sticks and small rocks aplenty, but if he felt any he gave no indication. When he reached the fence between our place and Mr Jenkins's he stuck one foot in the wire halfway up and launched himself up and over awkwardly, almost falling headlong when he landed. I clambered over in his wake, and at that point he did manage to pull away from me. I hit the ground just as he neared the house.

And then I was standing in Jenkins's kitchen. The pieces of the mug I had knocked to the floor were still there, dozens of sharp ceramic shards that were so much less than useful now. There was a small movement in the hall as a door closed the last few inches very slowly. At almost the same time, the outer kitchen door opened. There was a low squeal that was similar to the protests of our own misused screen door, and then my father slipped in on his bare and now very dirty feet. He was breathing hard, almost raggedly, but doing his best to keep it quiet.

"Dad!"

I could not help myself. "Dad, he's behind the door in the hall-way!"

My father looked around the kitchen with wide eyes while he tried to get his breathing under control. He started towards the hallway, stepping carefully around the sharp pieces of mug. I yelled again for him to watch out and when that didn't work, I ran towards him and put my hands up to push at him. Or I tried to. Just like with Mikey at the dam, I couldn't. It was not lethargy or any sort of external resistance, not even shitty blue twine. I willed myself to move, I begged myself, but I just didn't. The passivity of a dream momentarily took over, and I could only watch as my father moved into the hallway. I wanted to scream again. I wanted to grab him. I wanted to tell him I wished it had been me in the dam, and then all this would not be happening. Instead I watched as he walked by the door that Jenkins must have been behind.

Nothing happened.

He passed by and kept moving towards the door that might lead to me. I waited for Jenkins to emerge behind him, for something horrible to happen. My father reached the door and pushed it open.

"Caleb?" he whispered, peering into the darkness.

"Dad," I groaned from behind him. At the same time Jenkins emerged from the other door. In one hand he held a steak knife, and he looked…resigned. He walked forward quite normally, his feet making almost no sound in his thin slippers. Almost no sound. There was the slightest scuff, and my father turned from the door, his eyes widening, his thin chest rising as he started to draw in air to yell. But Jenkins was close and surprisingly fast. He took one more step and stuck the steak knife into my father's chest to almost three quarters of its length. Like I said, the little old man was strong. My father grunted and stepped back. Jenkins pulled the knife out with a jerk and sunk it in again, not quite as deeply this time. Blood spurted and hit Jenkins in the face, and he made that tsking sound again as he pulled the knife out once more.

"No! Dad!" I screamed. My father reeled at the top of the stairs, on the edge of the dark. I thought he would fall but then he kind of lurched forward and to one side. At the same time, Jenkins went to stick the knife in a third time and completely missed. He teetered himself, there in the doorway. I'd like to say my father pushed him but all that really happened was my father slumped slowly to the floor. Jenkins, our kind, quiet neighbour who had apparently been kidnapping and burying people in his hell room for God knows how long, evading suspicion and injury both, simply overbalanced and went headfirst into the dark. There came a shout and a couple of meaty thumping sounds, and then nothing.

15

I almost heaved again on waking but didn't quite get all the way there. Then I tried to spit the damn chemical taste out of my mouth before I remembered it was either that or the stench of wet dirt and rotting flesh. I was still lying on my side, my cheek pressed against the grit of the cold dirt floor, but I could see more than before—in the upper corner of my vision I could just make out that the door at the top of the stairs was now wide open. I tried to sit up. The room spun and I almost gagged, but after slumping back down and hitting my head on the floor twice, I managed to strain into a sitting position. The twine around my legs bit deep and even more painfully, but the couple of thin strands around my wrists actually seemed to have a little bit of give.

"Caleb."

It was very soft. I tried to ignore the sway and dip of the room as I looked towards the light of the doorway again. Dad.

I forgot I was tied up and tried to lurch to my feet. I flopped down again, my shoulder digging into the floor, and found myself staring at Jenkins. He was laying at the bottom of the stairs. He may not have broken a hip, but one leg was bent impossibly sideways. I doubted he had felt it, though. He stared at me, his eyes wide and unblinking, his forehead pushed both in and up at the same time. He would not be putting me in the dam, and he would not be putting anyone else in his wall of protruding hands.

"Caleb?"

Although it carried down to me, it seemed barely more than the idea of a whisper now.

"Dad!" I called, my own voice hoarse and breaking. "I'm here!"

I jerked myself forward, not thinking of anything beyond the need to get to him. I kind of flopped forward and had the strongest memory of the times Mikey and I would put ourselves in our sleeping bags and 'worm' around the lounge room, laughing at our own stupidity. I had been pretty good at it. On my second flop I landed next to our monster of a neighbour with his caved-in forehead, and I saw his steak knife still clutched in one hand, slick with my father's blood.

A couple more worm flops got me close enough to awkwardly slide my wrists over the knife.

"I'm coming," I called to my father. I had no idea if he heard me. I tried to jerk the twine backwards and forwards against the blade, but all I succeeded in doing was pushing the knife out of Jenkins's hand. So much for every movie, ever.

"I'm coming, I'm coming," I began repeating the words over and over as I grabbed at the knife with my bound hands and turned the blade inwards. I started sawing, managing only the smallest amount of pressure. I had to get to my father. I had seen the depth of both stabbings, and that spurt of blood that had arced across Jenkins's face. My sawing became more frantic. I sliced the meaty pad under one thumb, and then the side of my wrist, but I didn't let up. It felt like it took forever but I don't think it was actually very long. It was only twine, after all, and even Jenkins had decided he needed more of it before moving me. The twine parted and with my hands released it was easy enough to cut my legs free. It was painful to stand, but I managed to shuffle around Jenkins and get up the rest of the stairs without falling over.

My father was slumped against the wall exactly as I had seen — like I had seen Mikey's gouge marks in the mud, and like I had seen the dead claw of a hand sticking out of Jenkins's wall. I dropped to my knees next to him. He had a lot of blood down his front, bright red against his pale skin. There were two wounds where the knife had gone in — small, almost inconsequential-looking things. One wept blood, while the other had more of a stream flowing from it. For a second I thought he was dead, but then he drew a shallow breath. Red bubbles came out of the second knife hole. He raised one hand a little and opened one eye.

"Jenkins..." he began, and his eye rolled towards the dark doorway.

"He's dead," I cried. "He's dead. Oh, Dad."

"Caleb," Dad whispered, and then coughed another bright red bubble of blood. "Felt...felt so bad. I should - " He broke off and coughed hard for a second. A fine spray of blood hit me in the face, and when I wiped it away, I saw a red bubble hanging on his lip. His eye rolled and then focused on me again, and I saw something between amazement and horror on his too-white face. "Dreamed. You. Jenkins. Dead hands."

My father had dreamed of me in the room with Jenkins. He had seen those hands, rotten and protruding from the wall in claws, in surrender, in supplication. Maybe he had even heard the cheerful ramblings of Jenkins. It had not happened to him straight after Mikey's funeral like it had with me, but in the end the guilt had ripped him from his safe world. No, it wasn't just delayed guilt. I had done this to my father, I realised.

All alone, every afternoon.

Where were you, Dad?

He coughed again and then forced his other eye open.

"Phone, Caleb. Call an ambulance."

I hesitated, and he made a very small shooing gesture with one hand.

"Go. I'm…okay." And he smiled, just a little.

He did not sound okay, and he did not look okay, but I stood and ran to find the phone. There were a few frantic minutes in which I blubbered and fumbled through both the kitchen and the dark lounge room before I thought to switch on a lamp on a side table. As the light blinked on I had a bad moment when I was so certain Jenkins would be standing next to me that I almost screamed, but the only thing I saw was the phone. I dialled triple zero and asked for an ambulance to Jenkins's address, and said that my father was hurt and bleeding, that someone else was dead. I hung up without saying anything else. This was Cooing—someone being dead was a big deal. I knew that better than most. They would be here quickly, and one look at Jenkins's wall would bring in more adults. Plenty of them, I was sure. And I wanted to get back to Dad, not talk on the phone in a murderer's silent lounge room in the middle of the night.

"They are coming," I gasped out as I knelt back down by him.

He didn't say anything. His eyes were open, but he was not looking at me. The bubble of blood hung on his lower lip, poised and quivering for a second, and then it popped.

He was dead.

16

Cooing is famous, now. They called him the Wall Killer—not very imaginative, but the story has more than enough gruesome details to make up for that. I don't know how the town took it, in the long run. I have not been back there for a long time.

I spent a bit of time staying with Miss Abinathy down the road. It was not what a traumatised boy needed, but that is probably being very unfair. She took me in and tried to shield me from what was happening as best she could. Maybe she felt some obligation, given her—let's call it *association*—with my father. It did seem that she barely noticed the small additional weight of me, most probably because she was dealing with her own grief and shock. There was plenty to go around, particularly the shock. It moved through the town and out into the wider world like ripples from one of those stones I had thrown into the dam. The town swelled with reporters and the morbidly fascinated groups that were not always mutually exclusive. There was coverage, and images of the wall being carefully excavated, and pieces in the papers and on the internet covering the different victims, once they were identified. Young, old, men, women, teenagers. From three different states, from different cities and large towns, taken from streets and roadsides and campsites. No children, though. I don't think Jenkins was squeamish—but he was careful. Missing children attract a lot of attention. He knew that, and I was finding it out too. I even saw images of myself on the television, shaky footage taken at a distance, of me sitting at Miss Abinathy's dining room table, staring at nothing.

I had lost Mikey, and I had lost my father, and when I managed a few hours' sleep here and there, more of a collapse into exhaustion than anything planned or hoped for, I did not rest. I dreamed of Mikey drowning, and my father coughing bubbles of blood. I dreamed of dead hands protruding from a dirt wall, rotting skin and broken nails and fine, frail bones. And while I woke screaming or sobbing or gasping in the dark, I also woke relieved. They were just dreams, the pallid facsimiles of memory designed to remind me of my own guilt. I may not have been Jenkins, but I was not faultless.

I live far away now. I live with my uncle. He arrived after a series of mundane travel delays to take on a much larger burden than he had expected.

My uncle is kind despite how I have upended his life. Sometimes I catch him looking at me with questions in his eyes, but I am not sure if they are questions for me, or for himself. He probably wonders how he found himself in such a position— fettered by the son of his long-gone sister, dealing with horrors and family death by proxy. I guess he probably has at least a few very specific questions he has not yet dared to ask. Questions about that room, about Jenkins.

I was going to put you in the wall.

I still dream of Mikey, and Jenkins, and my father. I still dream of hands, and the smell of that room. And if I sometimes dream of what might be new darkness and images that hint at other horrible things, I do not speak of them. I don't get to choose what I dream, but I can choose what I say, and what I do not. I have my own grief and my own guilt, and now I fear both are far too easy to pass on.

All alone.

Where were you, Dad?

Publication History

A Good Big Brother (First published in Spawn: Weird Horror Tales About Pregnancy, Birth and Babies. IFWG, Australia, May 2021) Winner 2021 Australasian Shadows Award. Finalist for 2021 Ditmar Award.

Monstrous Behaviour (First published in *Etherea Magazine*, Issue 10, May 2022)

Memories of Blue (First published in *Daily Science Fiction*, June 2021)

Wriggleteeth (Original to collection) Honourable mention, AHWA short story competition 2023.

Dead-Go (First published by *Arcanist*, October 2022) 1st place, Arcanist Halloween flash competition 2022

Trial by Fire (First published in Etherea Magazine, Issue 18, 10 Oct 2023) Finalist Aurealis Award 2023. Finalist Ditmar Award 2023.

A Tomorrow With You In It (First published in *Cossmass Infinties*, Issue 9. July 2022)

Renting Space (First published in *The NoSleep Podcast*, Season 16 Episode 1 April 2021). Honourable Mention, AHWA short story competition 2019

The Cogwork Mermaid (Published in Etherea Magazine, October 2022)

Beach Memories (First published in *The NoSleep Podcast*, Season 18 Episode 6 August 2022) Finalist Aurealis Award 2022

Guess Who's Coming To Christmas Dinner? (First published in *The NoSleep Podcast*, Season 17 Episode 7 December 2021)

On The Big Screen (First published in *Scary Snippets Family Edition*, Nocturnal Sirens Publishing, 2020)

Jericho And The Cursed Forest (Original to collection)

Familiar (Original to collection)

There are Things on Me (First published in *Killer Creatures Down Under: Horror Stories with Bite*. IFWG International May 2023) Finalist Aurealis Award 2023. Finalist Ditmar Award 2023.

The Taste of Immolation (Original to collection)

Death Meets Noel Samuelson (To be published 2023 in Conflux 17 programme). 1st place, Conflux 16 short story competition 2022.

Sleep, Empty (First published in The NoSleep Podcast, Season 21, Episode 11, July 2024) Finalist 2024 Australasian Shadows Award

The Past Laid Out On The Table First published in *Cast of Wonders* Episode 506, September 2022) Finalist Aurealis Award 2022

Drowning In The Dark (Original to collection)